WELCOME TO THE WORLD OF
HOUSE SECRETS

This book is the second of the House Secrets series and takes place after both As Dawn Breaks and The Sorcerer's Touch. There exists a parallel between that House Secrets and the Blood Secrets trilogy as this is a *continuation*.

While the book *can* be read on its own, there are concepts and people in the Blood Secrets series and As Dawn Breaks which clarify some of the action in this story. It is recommended that you read those books first. However, I will include a brief introduction to the world, explain who is who on the introduction pages following and include a glossary of commonly used terms.

HOUSE SECRETS

how many secrets are hidden from view?

Immortal Consequences

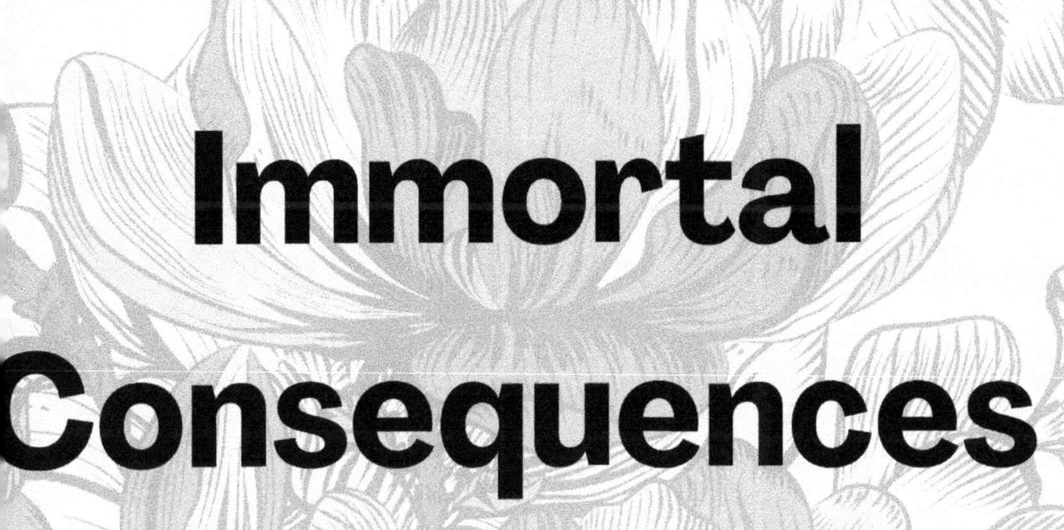

House Secrets
Book Two

Imogene Nix

Paperback ISBN 978-1-922369-30-7

Ebook ISBN 978-1-922369-29-1

Edited by: Hot Tree Editing

Cover by: Dexpress Covers

Please note:

The UK and USA share the English language, but there are many words that are spelled differently. Some words have extra letters in the British spelling, such as the word cancelled. In American English, it is spelled canceled. There are also words that interchange the letters c or s and sometimes z. For example, in America, you spell offense and in Britain, it is written as offence.

Examples of words you'll see in the book include: kerb, litre, centre, manoeuver, travelling and colour.

These spellings are **not** incorrect.

This book is written in UK English to reflect my Australian/English background.

INTRODUCTION

As the continuation of the Blood Secrets trilogy, some readers may come into the series, unknowing of what has gone before. This is a brief overview of The Blood Bride, The Illuminated Witch and The Sorcerer's Touch to assist you to understand the world you are entering.

In *The Blood Bride* we meet Hope, daughter of the House and Xavier, the Vampire Master of the House of Tudor. He's old and she's very young, returning to a divided house where her father holds the title of *Yeux Secondes*. Her brother, David and parents are hostile, but neither quite as much as Alexa—David's wife.

We learn about a secret in Hope's blood which makes her a valuable asset and on more than one occasion the bad guys try to abduct her.

On returning from College she meets Xavier and is fascinated, but so is he. After an attack she is taken below stairs, into the vampire accomodation for safety and one thing leads to another and Xavier and Hope fall in love.

After an attack, Xavier is injured and she ends up feeding him and she becomes a vampire when things go a little far. She learns to stand on her own two feet and is now a formidable figure, just as we learn about the Alpha Vamp — Attar.

In *The Illuminated Witch*, we first meet Celina, our witchling orphan, except she doesn't know she's a witch. When illness strikes her down in front of the House of Tudor office building, she meets Javed, second vampire of the house, who will soon be invested with his own nest.

Her magic is swelling and dangerous and she needs assistance, the kind that comes with training. But along the way, there is danger.

As with Hope, she too falls for the Master of this new house but things aren't straight forward. She's abducted and when Javed finds her, she's close to death. He turns her but not before they also finds three children among the many abductees. When Celina and Javed finally reunite as Vampires, they decide they will adopt the three girls —Lucy, Rachel and Marian. Though they aren't actually blood siblings, they've survived together for years and don't want to be split up.

In *The Sorcerer's Touch*, Daniel joins Hope and Celina in making the choice to turn. He's fallen for Mistress Vampire Cressida and is willing to give up everything for honour, duty and ultimately love.

Cressida and Hope end up adopting orphan nestling, Samantha as their daughter after an attack on another nest.

Together Hope and Xavier, Celina and Javed and Daniel and Cressida must fight the Alpha Vampire Attar, just as was foretold by the three women who are related to Attar, and turn up in all three books—Jemima, Daniella and Danicka.

GLOSSARY OF TERMS

Consort The unofficial partner of a Master or Mistress

House The formal name for a nest - eg *The House of Tudor*

Life Partner The official partner of a Master of Mistress

Lycans Weres of any variety

Master The male head of a House

Mistress The female head of a House

Nest A formal title for a house of vampires

Nestling One who chooses to live within a vampire nest

Second The vampiric second of the Master/Mistress of a house.

Yeux Secondes The title bestowed on the human head of a house. Meaning 'second eyes' and equivalent to the Second.

Why not subscribe to

Imogene **Nix's** newsletter?

http://bit.ly/INixNews

CHAPTER 1

Simon Bellingham prowled the hall, frustration washing over him since the phone call from Genevieve.

"We have a problem." Four small words, but they barely described the fury and horror. Julien was a problem. Working hand in hand with a band of unknown murderers, the lycan had created a much bigger issue. Simon's people had been outed against their will.

Knowledge of the responsibility he bore as Lord of Lycans weighed heavily on his shoulders.

"Simon, lover?" Cara, his current bed partner, called from within the "boudoir," as she continued to call it.

"I'll be there in a moment." He dragged a hand through his hair, aware that he needed to deal with this mess.

He'd hoped the vampires' victory over Attar would bring a sense of peace. It appeared the removal of one evil left an opening for another to rise.

Julien. He'd have to deal with him.

Cara edged around the door frame. "Come back to bed, lover. I'm hungry."

A hint of frustration wound through him. Cara had become clingy and irritating in her desire to push him to commit to her.

He'd enjoyed the dalliance. The sex was hot. A she-wolf who had no fears of procreation without the ritual. She was inventive. Gymnastic even from time to time, but that was palling.

"Cara, I've got a situation…"

"That's always your excuse." She pouted. "I'm ready and hot for you."

He grunted. "This isn't working, Cara."

Her eyes widened. "What? I think you may need to reconsider what you just said."

Simon grimaced as her words dripped with frigidity. But she was impeding his role. "Cara, I can't. We can't. You're wonderful. Witty, beautiful, and exciting, but I have competing responsibilities. My people and role must come first. I'm sorry."

Fury dawned on her face. "You fucking moron! I've given you my all. Devoted myself to keeping you satisfied, and this is it?" She flung her hand into the air. "I expected you to mate with me. To name me your consort!"

"I won't lie to you, Cara. I have responsibilities. You're lovely, but not the person I will take to consort. I made that clear at the beginning." And indeed he had. When they'd entered this relationship, he'd told her clearly that this wasn't love or ever after. He'd taken great care to ensure there were no false understandings. Whatever she had in her mind, she'd dragged it together all by herself.

She whirled into the bedroom, a tornado of snarling disappointment. She dragged clothes over her nude body while Simon watched her. Finally clothed, she tore the few items she'd hung in his cupboard from their hangers and stashed them in the large tote bag at the bottom of the storage unit, then marched to the bathroom.

Simon sighed. "I'll need your key too," he mumbled.

She snarled, reaching into her bag and tugging her keychain from the depths. Sliding it from the ring, she shoved it at his chest.

Her eyes, usually a soft blue, shone like pale sapphires. "You're a bastard, Lord of Lycans. One of these days, you'll face a threat, and I'll rejoice when you're removed from the position," she hissed and then slammed her way from his house.

He moved through the house to his office. It wasn't large, unlike the mansions the vampires inhabited with their humans. Lycans preferred family homes, somewhere small enough to suit a nuclear family, and this one served his needs.

He dragged the laptop from beneath the sheaves of paper and booted it up. He'd never really taken to them, but it was the only way to make it in this century, he had concluded.

Lycans might live hundreds of years, but they weren't like the vamps, with corporations and nests that spanned generations. Instead, they lived in small groups, some off the grid while others made it through as mechanics, plumbers, and there was more than one doctor and dentist he could name.

He brought up the program that would allow him to talk face to face with his mentor, the man he'd succeeded as the Lord of Lycans. His grandfather, Frederick.

He didn't look a day over fifty, and if Simon hadn't known better, he would never have believed the man was approaching his five-hundredth birthday.

"Yo! Lord of Lycans. It's wonderful to see your face."

Simon blinked. "Hi, Gramps. I need some advice."

His grandfather paused for a moment, searching Simon's face before turning around. "Take the kids outside, honey, and I'll be with you shortly."

"How's Marta coping?" Simon asked once his grandfather faced the screen again.

Frederick grunted. "She's finding it hard. Your newest aunt is teething, and Bernard refuses to do his reading after school."

Simon laughed. Incongruous as it may be, after the death of his grandmother, Elinore, Frederick had mated twenty years ago. He and Marta were now the proud parents of five-month-old Sharna, six-year-old Bernard, and ten-year-old twins Marla and Ned.

"I wish Dad could have seen them."

Frederick grunted. "He'd have complained every time one of them burped on his shoulder or got off with his hats."

Simon laughed. "True."

"So tell me. What's the problem?"

Simon shook his head. "I've got this half-shifter woman and her mate. They're planning to join the pack, but she's got a ghost in the cupboard, I guess you might say. An upstart from one of the southern packs, and he's troublesome."

Frederick tapped a hand on the table. "And?"

"Julien has been running with an unknown crowd. He's somehow involved in the murders of several servants of unhoused vamps."

"Hand it over to the vamps, then."

Simon winced. "It's not quite that simple. They're stretched, and while their team brought down Attar—the murderous freak vamp— they need my assistance. They actively requested it through Genevieve's mate."

"Through her mate?" The words were low and full of disbelief.

Unable to contain the sigh, Simon nodded. "He was a *Yeux Secondes.*"

Frederick inhaled. "Boy, what are you mixed up in?"

"Normally, I would let the Liaison Division and the vamp Council deal with it, but we've got a lycan at the centre of this mess." He shook his head, feeling very unsure of what he should do.

"You need an investigator. Someone with connections."

"You know someone, Gramps?"

Frederick blinked. "I may do. Let me reach out to them, ask, and if they're amenable, I'll have them contact you."

"Thanks. You better go help Marta now."

Frederick barked a laugh. "Ha! It's your turn now. Any female who appeals?"

Simon grimaced. "No. I just ended it with Cara."

Frederick sighed. "She won't have taken that well. I know her type. Pretty, but wanted to tie you up in a bow you didn't want, right?"

"Something like that. Anyway, I better get some sleep. It's getting late."

Frederick laughed. "And the day is still young here. Simon, you know I'm proud of you. The man you've become. The leader. Your father would be too."

The words pierced him. He barely remembered his parents, as they'd perished along with his younger brother in a house fire.

"That means a lot." He touched the screen, thankful his grandfather still had many years left. "I gotta go."

He disconnected between them, then sat there in the gloom, looking at the screen.

*N*iamh waited until the lights went out, then stretched and opened the front door. If only she could live openly, but the world wasn't yet ready for her kind to appear. So instead, she remained hidden from earthly view. She wore a uniform she'd customised for her size and specific requirements; unlike the sparkle of blond in her hair and the mischievous lights in her green eyes, the dull greyish blue was drab.

In the depths of the night, tugging her jacket around herself, concealing her wings, Niamh skipped out into the street.

Working in an alien environment wasn't quite how she'd seen her life unfolding, but fates were fickle. She'd been sent far away from the land of her birth. She'd hoped to make a new life, and she was coping. Barely, but she was learning the strange ways of the Americans. It hadn't been her choice, but she would make the best of it.

Footsteps echoed behind her, and she looked for somewhere to hide, but the jungle of suburbia wasn't filled with trees or green spaces where she might blend in. Not for the first time, she wished she could return to Ireland, but Niamh had been banished until she could prove able to provide for herself. And everyone knew opportunity knocked in the colonial countries, didn't they? Her cousin, Iona, had settled in Australia and was working on a large cattle station, well at home among the cattle and large open areas.

Making herself settle to the matter at hand, Niamh loosened the carefully altered uniform sleeves under her jacket, ready to divest it should she need to.

It paid to be prepared in the city, Niamh reminded herself. She kept moving, but tension wound around her.

In the large window opposite, she caught sight of a man loping close behind. Something about his attitude told her he was full of menace.

At the brush of a hand, she gasped, slid free of her coat, and unfurled her wings. She rose, allowing her wings to beat furiously while she turned in mid-air.

Her attacker's face was obscured at the height she'd achieved, But his anger battered at her as she zoomed up and away.

CHAPTER 2

Fury scorched deep.

She'd escaped him.

The woman he'd been hunting, following to the hospital. She carried the scent of paranormal about her. Likely yet another servant, ergo expendable. They all were. He'd starve them until they could no longer cope. Then he'd offer them a deal.

He'd protect them from the vamps and the pack. They'd become his puppets and would do his bidding.

Sniffing the air again, his mind splintered and rebounded back to the initial question.

How had she eluded him? She'd disappeared from his view, and he'd been left with her coat. One second there and then the next gone.

He pulled it close and noted the arms flapped wide. As if she'd prepared for such an attack. That had him frowning.

"How does this even happen?" Had someone tipped her off? But no, he hadn't uttered a word of his grand plan to anyone. Not even his family, who supported his push to assume control.

His mind blurred. He'd been in that half state between human and something else. The one he assumed at the time of a kill.

Denied.
Hungry.
He'd hunt again.
Soon.

CHAPTER 3

The hospital was sprawling, with glowing lights, but Niamh kept her distance. She should have been at work, but without her jacket, entering with her wings exposed would announce to one and all that another kind of paranormal lived here.

She slumped onto a seat and dug deep into her bag.

Perhaps her friend Ellen might drop a cape around? She pressed the buttons on the phone and waited out the ringing signals.

"Yeah? What's wrong, hon?" The gravelly voice settled her jangling nerves.

"I need help. Someone was going to hurt me, and I had to lose my jacket and escape. Do you have a cape I could borrow until I—"

"Now who on earth would want to hurt an itty-bitty thing like you?" Fear filtered into Niamh's brain as she heard Ellen's query.

"I don't know. I was just leaving home when—"

"Home? Does someone know where you live? Where are you now? Somewhere safe?"

Niamh glanced around the park, deserted and dark. At least she hoped so. But with the number of paranormals in the area, you could never be sure.

"I'm in the park opposite the hospital."

"I'll be right there. On the bench by the entry?"

"Yes."

The call disconnected, and Niamh took a breath, though it was unsteady. At least Ellen understood the problem. She'd been Niamh's contact when she'd first come to this land of vast concrete edifices and buildings. She was also the supervisor of her shift, so ringing Ellen actually took two things off her plate, explaining why she'd be late for her shift and telling her that likely Niamh's location and status were breached.

Niamh peered at the lights and could make out a woman hurrying across the street. Ellen was almost as slight as she was, an older member of the clan she'd left. In each generation there were those who were sent away, either to make a new life or because they couldn't conform. For Ellen, she'd actively campaigned to be released from the place she'd been birthed, wanting more and bigger.

"Here." Ellen thrust the cape into her hands. "You best come now, though, because I hear there's going to be an inspection tomorrow morning, and they want the entire women's ward in B5 ready to go through."

The hospital was being rehabilitated, and they were regularly given only a day's notice to bring wards and entire areas up to scratch before inspections were held.

She slid the material around her shoulders. "Thanks, Ellen. I can stay back if needed."

The woman shook her head. "No. You'll be taken home tonight by Maxim." Even before Niamh could open her mouth, the woman shook her head as they scurried towards a concealed entrance. "We can't have you being endangered. Yer mam would have my guts for garters."

Niamh nearly laughed, but her mother was not a woman to be trifled with, so she accepted the words, knowing she'd take Ellen to task if something did indeed happen to her offspring.

In the changing room, she hurried about fixing her wings so they were out of view, then grabbed the cleaning trolley she'd been assigned, and Ellen gave her specifics of the tasks she must accomplish.

*S*imon woke to the hammering of his front door and the harsh burning sunlight on his face.

"What the...?" He glanced at the clock beside the bed and jack-knifed up. "Fucking hell!" The alarm hadn't gone off, and his first appointment of the day would arrive in under fifteen minutes. If he didn't miss his guess, the knocking was likely his assistant, Jessica, wondering why the door wasn't unlocked for her to enter.

Thankful he'd thought to don at least light boxer-style pyjama bottoms, he strode to the door and pulled it open. Her eyes widened.

"A bit late for those, don't you think?" She brushed past him. "I'll get the coffee on and start the machine while you shower and dress."

He rubbed his hands through his hair and grunted before turning and slamming his bedroom door.

Less than ten minutes later, he'd managed a quick shower, thanked the heavens he'd invested in a woman to iron for him and clean, and looked at himself in the mirror. He was lean and tall, his face chiselled in the jaw and his eyes a deep blue. He knew he still carried the English accent, a holdover from infancy in 1800 England. His grandfather had brought the entire clan to America in early 1804, and they'd weathered the many storms by taking refuge in the country's north. His grandfather had since returned to the clan holdings in northern England with his new family.

"Are you ready, Simon? You have a meeting in five minutes," Jessica called.

Of course he did. Genevieve Fernly and David had requested the meeting the night before, and he'd messaged Jessica to warn her to prepare.

Exiting the room, he'd barely set himself down in the armchair when he heard the peal of the bell. Jessica hurried in, the couple following her.

David reached out his hand, still new to the were aspect of life; he didn't realise the deference of one were to another, especially a more highly ranked male, meant he was to wait.

Genevieve grimaced, and Simon laughed loudly. "It's okay. Take a seat."

He watched David's furtive glance to Genevieve.

"You can explain later. But show me this note," Simon said.

Genevieve tugged a small bagged piece of paper from her pocket and handed it over.

Genevieve, ma coeur.

I never meant to keep these things, but you know shifters and our need to keep trophies. Like your mother and that coin. Yes, I know about it and your father. Such a shame that you will lose everything because she had to have a one-night stand.

I would have taken you away from all that confusing human trash. I planned to make you mine, then fight for control of the pack. Then you chose him, and my plans came to naught.

So, I guess this is your mess to clean up.

Me, well, I'm leaving town. Going to find somewhere to howl and enjoy the spoils of hunting. Somewhere far, far away. Now you can chase me. You can try, but dearest, you don't have the nose for this kind of hunt. I'd tell you to give it all up, but you won't.

I'm counting on that.

By the way, your new man may be a shifter, but he has no training. No knowledge of the magic and wonder we can instil. He'll never survive in a pack because you're an abomination against my kind. You should give him up now, before it's too late and he crosses some line and must face the trials. Because he simply won't survive.

Ah well. Your choice.

I won't bid you goodbye, simply adieu.

Julien

He read the words. Considered them and the underlying thread of hate. "Nice guy."

She blushed with embarrassment. "I... He isn't mine."

No. That much was clear from the missive. But he had been. Once. "I'll need to visit the pack. See if they can tell me where he's gone."

Her lips thinned. "I doubt they'll tell you anything. The pack isn't exactly warm and welcoming."

"So, tell me what you know."

David blinked. "I'm not sure there's much to tell. You've read the note. Genevieve had a relationship with him when she was younger. His intention was to use her to gain control of the pack. He moved here in the recent past, created difficulties for her at work, and now he's making threats."

Simon waved his comments away. He needed to hear from Genevieve first. Then he'd sort out the mess of how he'd track the mongrel down.

"Genevieve?"

She shrugged. "It's pretty close to what David said. You know my background. My mother and her wild ways. She was in contact with Julien's family until this happened. And no, I haven't told her about this letter or his actions. That would be a step too far right now." She glanced at him. "She's convinced I should mate with him. I've not yet told her it's too late. I know Julien's in touch with his family, but knowing him, I doubt he's told them where he's hunkering down. Only that he has a plan and will bring them into it when he's good and ready. They doted on him. His father is the beta, and he's the only son. All their other offspring are daughters, which won't bring them the glory they seek."

He grunted at the assessment of the situation. He'd dealt with others like this before. Messy backgrounds, those who felt disenfranchised yet hadn't the ability to step up and take control of their packs.

"All right. Do you have any idea where he might have gone?"

She shook her head. "No. None of this makes sense. I know he had a place on the south side. I've been in touch with the lieutenant, and he sent someone over there, but it's cleared out. He's gone into the wind. He sold his vehicle too."

Now he frowned. "Sold the car?"

"He doesn't want us to find him. I can put out a BOLO, but he'd be expecting that," she added.

"No. We don't want to tip him off just yet. And you're sure that handwriting is his?"

Genevieve nodded.

"Lord... uh..." David cleared his throat, clearly having now caught on that his earlier overture wasn't what was expected.

"'Simon' is fine, David. The vamps have no information?"

He shook his head. "They're unable to assist in this matter right now. Not because they don't want to, as Cressida tasked me with telling you they'll do all they can, but they're still recovering. Attar took a toll they didn't expect. We..." He stopped himself as if he wrestled inwardly. "The houses have no one to offer for a little while. Once they're at full strength again, however, Cressida and the Council wish to meet with you to formalise an agreement between any paranormals that exist. They understand that protection of those weaker than them will require a broader view. She's been given the power to make this happen."

Simon weighed the words. He knew Cressida, an aged and powerful vampire, had recently become the liege of the vampires. He'd been unaware that they'd been discussing this, since his grandfather had made overtures in the fifties and sixties to form just such an alliance.

"That's an offer I will look into. Once we get through this current crisis."

Niamh couldn't believe her luck. The area she'd been designated to clean was empty of all furniture, so she hurried to ensure the floors were clean. Next she scrubbed the walls before beginning on the ablution area.

By the time her shift ended, it shined like a new five pence piece. Stretching her back, she waited for the customary crack while the pressure on her spine abated.

"You've done excellent work," Ellen said, checking out the area with a slow and methodical eye.

Niamh jumped. "You frightened me!"

The older woman simply smiled in response. "You do very good work, Niamh. At this rate, they'll want you on the day shift, and I'm not sure I could keep you here. But this… is it what you envisaged when you came to America?"

"It's not what I expected I'd be doing. But I have to eat until I can either return home or find something else a little less stressful to do. Or study." Not that she was complaining. Ellen had taken her on with no experience, taught her the job, and given her an opportunity. She'd be eternally grateful for the start, but she needed better if she had any hopes of being able to return to the country of her birth.

"You've done well, child. But there are bad things around here, things that will gobble you up as soon as look at you, as you know. Tonight…" Ellen shivered, her eyes wide. "I've made arrangements. Maxim will take you home, and I need you to be careful. I've heard even the vamps aren't safe right now."

A shock of fear slid through her, like a worm through soil might, with undulations. "What do you mean? Ellen, the vamps and weres are the strongest of—"

The sound of footsteps echoed. "Shh…"

Maxim lumbered in. He too was a fairy, though from another glade. He'd been banished because he'd made the mistake of wanting to be with a nymph against the wishes of his kind. She'd not known him before. Ellen had said he'd been here for some time, and she'd never known him as anything other than the lonely man who stood before them, sad and insular.

Not for the first time, she wished someone could breach that cloud he seemed to fold around himself. The one that stopped anyone getting close. As with many of their number who'd been sent away—and anyone who knew the fairy leaders understood conflict was not their way—he'd had to reinvent himself. He looked maybe thirty in human years, with a sad smile, long brown hair he wore in a tail, and trim though tall of stature.

She smiled, pleased that they would make their way to the

changing rooms together. It felt like some kind of discordant family. "Hey, Maxim, maybe we should grab a bite to eat on the way home?"

He turned and shook his head. "I'll drop you off before I go home." His voice was heavily accented, betraying his Russian ancestry.

Ellen had explained he'd already been here ten years and learned English because he'd intended to blend in. But the sad cloud seemed to put paid to that attempt, she thought. How could anyone that alone possibly blend into a crowd?

They climbed into his car, and he drove sedately, taking great care to make sure they arrived in one piece before he pulled in by her home.

At the door, she looked back, but he waited patiently in the car to see her enter. Sighing, Niamh turned, slid the key into the lock, and stepped inside.

With a flick, the lights illuminated the small apartment. It wasn't much. One room was sectioned into multiple uses as a bedroom, lounge, and kitchen, but at least there was a tiny cupboard-like bathroom. She didn't need to share.

Sliding the bolt of the front door into place, she exhaled and stripped off the borrowed cape. Tomorrow she'd need to purchase a new jacket to replace the one she'd lost, then make the necessary alterations. It would mean dipping into her emergency funds, but that was what they were for.

Niamh tottered to the bathroom, stripping as she went.

She turned the shower on, then dumped her clothes into the miniscule hamper. "I'll need to launder tomorrow." The small line she strung up in the bathroom didn't allow for a lot, but she lived alone, and mostly the clothes she wore were the horrid uniform and old comfortable sweatpants with matching tops. She spent as much time during the daylight hours hiding away from the humans as possible. They had no idea fairies such as her even existed, and the unwritten though cardinal rule was to never tell. She adhered to that one studiously.

She had determined early on that food was easier when delivered, and on the odd occasion she left this place of safety, it was at night, when no one would get a glimpse of her shimmering wings. She always ensured they were hidden from sight in long jackets or dresses where she could conceal them.

Summer was a trial, with long days, short nights, and high temps, but she'd accepted that there was nothing more she could do.

Stepping under the water, she let the cares of the night wash away down the drain.

"I am calm. I am determined. I will make this life a success." The mantra soothed the last ragged edges of her anxiety away, as it always did.

Winding the towel around herself, she wiped away the moisture beading her body. The old spotted mirror above the sink showed the smudges below her eyes. The concave hollows beneath her cheekbones. Lips just a shade too wide and eyes that shone like emeralds. Her hair a ragged sweep of dirty blond. More than once, she'd wished for the rich, shimmery red curtain most of her cousins sported.

"If wishes were horses, my girl."

She towelled off and headed for the area she'd designated as the sleeping zone. The lounge chair was long enough to double as a bed, but opposite was the television, and she'd taken to finding a musical channel, sliding it down low so not as to disturb the neighbours.

The bottle of water she kept on the small battered coffee table that doubled as her dinner place was empty, so she turned to the kitchenette and filled it, ensuring to pull the blinds and curtains as she always did.

Finally assured of her privacy, she sipped and lay down.

Sleep captured her, and reality spun away.

CHAPTER 4

*S*imon waited anxiously for a call that didn't come. After two days, he was ready to climb the walls, as frustration ate away at him. Jessica told him more than once that Frederick would get back to him in his own time.

"Yes, I know. But I need to track down where the fuck Julien has gone."

Jessica grimaced. "I know. But neither of us has the experience, and from what you've shared of the letter, if you allow Genevieve to search for him, he'll do more than simply make her life a living hell. You endanger them both."

And there it was. The reason he refused to allow them to participate in the hunt. It wasn't like there weren't ample weres out there, wanting the opportunity to hunt down one of their kind who'd betrayed them. But they needed someone with experience. Someone who could finish it without alerting the human authorities. Someone other weres would obey without question.

"I can't do that. Now that they've integrated into the clan, it's my role to protect them. Yes, Genevieve is a cop, but that doesn't mean I can throw her out there to fend for herself and him." He rubbed his hands over his stubbled chin.

"Maybe you could contact him again?"

He grunted. He could, but Frederick was busy, and he knew, even if he called, until his grandfather had tracked down the person, he'd simply tell him to wait. And learn patience.

For some overwhelming reason, though, the urgency was building in Simon's veins. "So let's look at the documentation we've been sent. I'm not so sure that I like the idea of buying a block of units."

Jessica sighed and rolled her eyes. "Norman put up a very good argument. We have a lot of young and unattached paras in the city. They need homes. These units have a low occupancy rate, and by making them available, we ensure the cash flow for the pack. You said it yourself, Simon. We have to look at the issues logically. To remain a force, we need income. A portfolio. And this is a good entry-level option. Besides, we can start with humans first, if you're that bothered."

He rubbed his head. "Did the report on the condition come in? What about the list of current occupants?"

She shuffled through the mess on his desk. "You know, you need a wife to keep you tidy and on track. I gave it to you yesterday."

He huffed. "Why do I need a wife? I have a cleaner and you."

The smile she gave him was tight. "For now."

Simon frowned. "What's that supposed to mean?"

Jessica slid into the seat opposite him. "The cleaner is fine. She's one of us. But my role... I'm ready to find a mate, Simon. Someone who will fulfil me."

Blinking, he considered her words. "You want to be my consort?"

She reared back as if he'd stuck her with a knife. "No! God no! You're not the kind of person I'd..." Jessica cleared her throat. "I mean, you're my boss and my friend."

Relaxing, he laughed. "Okay, for a moment there I was a little scared."

He didn't duck fast enough, and she smacked him with the file in her hand.

"No. I just meant I'm ready to find a mate, but that means you'll need to look for a replacement for me. I can't do this forever, especially when…" Her words trailed away, but not before he got the gist of what she was edging around.

"Of course. But we've got a little time. So, while you're still here, we should get on with these negotiations." He took the file she held out and flipped it open. The buildings were in reasonable repair. There were only three tenants in the building that could house twenty-four. Most apartments were efficiency-style units. Single-roomed, though at least spacious enough to allow for some designations in the zones. Each had its own private bathroom. Upstairs were a few larger units. When he checked the income, he lifted his gaze. "What's the average income on a single-bedroom apartment in town?"

Jessica shrugged. "I have no idea."

"Look that up and get back to me. I want to know how the pricing of the tenancy stacks up before I make a final determination, and if I consider going ahead, I want to inspect them. A report can't explain subtleties, and I might pick up on something that's been missed."

"Sure thing, Simon." She rose, but before turning, she tapped her lips with her long scarlet fingernail. "You also wanted me to remind you a pack social is overdue. Choose a date and time. I'll hunt out a suitable location."

He rolled his eyes. Pack social indeed.

"Yeah, sure," he answered without any enthusiasm, and Jessica laughed as she retreated.

The jacket was a dark blue felt. "It's going to take some work," Niamh told herself, but it was the dragonfly motif on it that drew her eye.

Fairies didn't really have totems, not like natives of some cultures, but an affinity usually showed itself once the fairy had come of age. Hers was a dragonfly. Quick and lithe, bright and ultimately adaptable.

"And haven't I proved myself to be capable of change? Look, here I am in America. Doing it alone." She slid her finger over the motif, tracing the outline of the long body and double wings of iridescent thread. *So pretty.*

It had definitely stretched the budget, but the urge to purchase it when she'd seen it in the store had been strong.

Now she sat on her couch, gathering the sewing supplies her grandmother had gifted her upon leaving home. With careful moves, Niamh removed the threads at the arms, sliding the tiny thread cutter between the seams.

She stopped only for the bathroom and to drink water. By the time the light disappeared from the horizon, she'd made the new quick release fasteners an almost invisible part of the coat.

"There." Niamh sat back to consider her work. Every stitch even and hidden from view, it was as if the coat hadn't been altered. "Excellent."

Niamh set about clearing away the workbox and rose, heading for the kitchen when three rapid knocks caught her attention. "Just one moment," she called and used the small mirror she kept for this reason to ensure her wings were carefully hidden from view.

Sliding the door open only as far as the security chain allowed, she peered outside. "Yes?"

An envelope was thrust into her hands by the supervisor of the building. "An inspection is due by some guy who's planning on buying the building. All the information is inside."

"Oh. Thank you." She accepted the note and shut the door before the man could speak again. Not that she didn't wish to converse, but he was human, and the more she interacted, the higher the chance she might be outed. Not something she could afford.

With shaking fingers, Niamh broke the seal.

Attention Tenant:

This property is being inspected for sale to an investment company. Notice is hereby rendered that your apartment will be viewed tomorrow night at 6:30 p.m.

We request you make all necessary preparations for this event.

Should you not be on-site during the inspection, the supervisor will grant access to the inspector for the purposes of checking the integrity of the building. They will remain on-site to ensure the safety of your effects...

"Damn them." But there wasn't much she could do. She calculated how she might be there without taking a chance that they'd learn her secret.

Palming her mobile phone, she sent a text to Ellen. *<I've got a problem tomorrow night. They're inspecting my apartment as the building is for sale. I will be late. N xx>*

At least tonight was her weekend, so she'd have time to prepare. Cleaning wasn't so much the issue as finding spaces to place things she didn't wish humans to see, including her flower circlet presented at maturation and the formal gown that denoted her as fully grown. The green velvet gown had openings for her wings that were unmissable. There were also her tiny mementos, gifted to ensure she remembered ways and people. A rock with the kiss of a fairy wing impressed into it. A feather from a bird fairy she'd danced with.

She carefully collected them all together and slipped them into her suitcase, then slid it under the bed. No one would find them unless they rifled through her belongings.

Morning dawned, and she yawned, stretching, checking the area once again. Finally, pleased that everything was out of sight, she lay down and closed her eyes, allowing sleep to claim her.

Darkness filled Niamh's mind.

Evil scooting along the edges. Holding her captive. Her pulse skittered and tripped with fear.

"Where am I?" she called, but there was no answer. All before her were shades of grey and black. A reality she'd never seen or touched. It was so alien to the reds and greens she knew from home. Terror shot hard through her.

She reached out, fingers touching upon shadows that cut her till she bled, and she scooted back, hoping she'd find her way back to awareness and safety.

At the ends of her senses, she became aware something watched.

It wanted to devour her. To suck the life from her. To absorb the light that each fairy held inside themselves.

"I don't want to die. Please let me go," she called.

Laughter, raucous and infused with evil, echoed.

"Please," she entreated.

Her eyes flicked open, searching for and finding the alarm clock. Three o'clock in the afternoon.

She ran a shaking hand across her face, feeling the beaded moisture that gathered there, and noted the mess of her bed. The sheets were tangled and damp with perspiration.

"What the hell was that?" she whispered. She'd never encountered a nightmare before, the reality so alien. "I should tell Mam." But the truth of her situation blindsided her. She'd been sent away to learn to cope, to build a life. Calling home wasn't an option anymore. She'd been forbidden to make contact unless her life was under threat or her true identity in jeopardy.

"Just a nightmare," she told herself, rising and heading for the bathroom. "Perhaps I should raise it with Ellen?" But why would she? Nightmares were common among humans. They didn't pose any danger, did they? Humans survived them, and so would she.

Once she returned to the kitchen, she found the kettle and set it on the hob to boil. A cup of herbal tea might just settle her nerves.

That was what she needed. Not to set her concerns on her friend's shoulders.

But letting go of the darkness wasn't simple or easy.

The rest of the day passed as if someone were watching her, and her skin crawled so much that by the time six rolled around, she was a bundle of nerves.

The sound of a knock on her door had her jumping up, a quiver under the skin as nerves danced.

She reached out, smoothing the faded blue of her uniform down over her legs.

Before her stood the superintendent and another man. Imposing, with piercing eyes and a smile that sent her knees to jelly.

"We're here for the inspection."

he woman before them was tiny, her face fine, like the lines of her body contained in the ugly utilitarian uniform she wore.

"Come in." Her voice was rich with the strains of Ireland, the cadence slow, but on her face, he read concern and worry. She was trying to hide a deep emotion, and the wolf inside him scented it. Wanted to paw the ground and howl. He wrestled with the immediate response, holding it at bay. *Now isn't the time or the place.*

Simon entered the apartment. "We won't take long," he hurried to assure her.

Niamh Ryan, as the superintendent had called her, slid back from the door, her hands a flutter of terror that betrayed her Simon cast around for the right term. Terror came to mind, and his guts twisted.

His gaze travelled the tiny efficiency apartment. It was sparsely furnished. A single wardrobe and chest of drawers took up one wall along with a television. A three-seater couch and a coffee table. No dining zone, though the kitchenette was immaculate but humble. The floors were the aged linoleum he guessed had been installed when the building was erected.

Every inch was spotless but bare of personality.

"Have you lived here long, Ms Ryan?"

She squeaked and jumped, and he frowned.

"Are you all right?"

"Oh, yes," she answered with a whisper, eyes downcast.

His eyes fluttered to the door, the chain and deadbolt along with the traditional lock little in the way of physical deterrents to someone truly intent on entering.

The walls appeared even and without the telltale cracks that would betray movement. The windows were secure and well maintained.

He stepped farther into the room, and she slid back. A greasy emotion akin to regret settled in his belly. "You've been here, what, six months?"

She nodded her answer as the superintendent looked on with a bored expression.

"Do you feel safe here?"

Now her eyes moved, and their gazes collided.

"I... I guess."

If anyone had told him he'd feel a zap of connection with some random woman in a single-room apartment he'd been inspecting for sale, Simon would have laughed them off. Until now, that was. Because it happened.

When her eyes widened, her lips opening to a silent *O*, he knew she'd felt it too.

Instinct drove him to thrust a hand deep into his pocket, pull out a card, and hand it to her. "Ms Ryan, here's my card. If you need anything, just call." It wasn't nearly enough, but he could scent her confusion. He wouldn't make it worse, because if he was reading the signs right, he'd found his mate.

Simon wanted to reach out, take her hand, but he read in her face that she'd be skittish, wouldn't accept the approach, so instead, he'd take his time. Far too many times he'd heard of those making a reckless advance only to be rebuffed. They'd lost their mates because they wouldn't and couldn't show patience and understanding.

I can give her the time and space. He nodded and watched as her gaze flicked from the card, then back to his face.

The superintendent cleared his throat. "All done?"

Simon cursed that the man had been there at their first meeting. "Of course," he answered smoothly and retreated, not that he wanted to.

Shifting his mind to business, he looked up, once again glancing at the facade. It was an older building, approximately forty years old, and in need of refurbishment. Would he make the purchase?

The building was in good repair. He'd had men in the ceiling, an electrician and plumber had been retained, but having contacted the company who'd maintained the building, all the information had built a picture of an excellent investment.

They trudged to the next small apartment, this one empty. As with all the others, it was efficient with the basics needed, but he didn't need to see any more. From this point on, it was simply going through the process.

At the end, he shook hands with the super and retreated to his vehicle, then lifted his cell to his ear. "Make the deal," he informed his lawyer.

"Yes, sir. How do you want to deal with the current tenants? Do you wish to evict and—"

In his chest, a bubble of frustration rose. "No. They remain."

He needed the woman, Niamh Ryan, to stay exactly where she was. Needed to know where to find her. Needed to ensure her safety.

"Okay. Anything else?"

The words echoed in his brain.

"Yeah. I want effective security put in place in the building. The super replaced with one of my people too. Make it happen, Belrose."

"Uh... sure," the man muttered.

Once that was in place, he'd give orders to make sure Ms Ryan was safe. It was all he could do for the moment. Not nearly enough, but he'd have to take it slow.

He didn't want to leave.

Simon gave the building a last longing glance before rolling into the flow of traffic.

CHAPTER 5

*J*ulia Cummings hurried up the street at ten o'clock at night. While it was late, it wasn't out of the ordinary for her to head home from work at this hour. "If only the boss hadn't wanted to work late, I'd be home, safe in my bed." She wasn't opposed to late nights, but usually she would be accompanied by some friends, wobbling down the street together after a grand time out.

Tonight was different, she thought, hurrying home after catching the train nearest to her house.

The night appeared dark and scarily dangerous.

Her heels clipped on the concrete, beating a rapid tattoo. She turned her head, searching over her shoulder. Was someone behind her?

The park lay ahead. She could hustle through there and be home in under three minutes. It might be dark, but she'd taken that shortcut before.

Edging past the old metal fence, she followed the path, the light in the centre of the park so far away.

Then she felt it, the whisper of air against the nape against her neck. Hot. Oppressive.

Her heart thudded in her chest.

Something brushed past her, and she stopped. "Who... who's there?"

Julia trembled, tugged her purse tighter against her body. The air wasn't cold, but there was a chilling finger sliding through her nerves.

"Hello?"

"Come to me."

The voice flitted through her brain. Demanding her presence.

Her feet moved even as she opened her mouth to scream.

Nothing came out as darkness descended.

CHAPTER 6

The local news was playing softly on the television when Niamh woke, and she glanced towards the electrical unit to see a reporter talking about a missing woman.

Her face flashed up on the screen as Niamh stretched, half listening.

"Julia Cummings was headed home from a late night. The last reported sighting was at the subway station..."

Niamh tuned out as she stood and stumbled to the kitchen. A cup of tea would set her to right. She'd wake and shower. A glance at the clock showed her there were still a couple hours to sunset. She'd make meals from the food she'd bought and stash them in the small freezer so she wouldn't need to worry for the next few days.

A knock at the door. Niamh scurried forwards, but an envelope was slid beneath it before she had time to turn the handle.

With care, she bent down and picked up the white packet, then retreated to the kitchen just as the kettle whistled.

She poured the water into the cup, letting it wash over the tea infuser, and picked at the envelope's closure. Inside lay a heavy piece of paper, and she slid it out, unfolding it so the embossed heading came into view.

You are advised that the building has been purchased... No change to your status as tenant or the agreement...

Taking the cup, Niamh headed to the lounge, wondering if the man who'd visited was the purchaser or simply an agent for some consortium. "Not really your problem, Niamh, my girl."

Reading further, she noted the superintendent would be changing. "Well, at least I'm staying. For now."

Not that she loved this apartment by any stretch, but until she found a better job, it was all she could afford.

Sipping her tea, she let her mind wander back to Ireland. The rolling hills of green, cool mornings, so fresh and crisp. Memories of the sounds of birds and insects as they chattered gaily.

Here in New York, there was the occasional pigeon, rat, or loose animal, but it wasn't the same. True, there was a vibrancy all its own, but different from home. She'd walked the parks at night. The great open spaces and the well-established trees and pathways.

"I wonder if I'll ever really settle here?"

She could contact the local fairies but hadn't so far because... "I want to go home."

Even that wasn't totally true. Going home wasn't possible. She'd been banished to America and had started coming to terms with that. But Niamh craved a home with green space around it. Privacy where hiding behind a door wasn't the only way to protect her secrets.

"And a proper bed." The couch was fine for now, but she longed for a bed she could make up and flop into with a book when the urge hit.

Instead of dwelling on what she didn't have, Niamh rose and started pulling her ingredients from the cupboard and fridge. "I will make this a positive," she told herself as she set about chopping up the ingredients.

But the whole time, in the back of her mind, the reality of her life played over and over again. The time had come to reconsider what she had, where she was going, and how to achieve those ends. If only a pair of shining eyes and a hint of a smile didn't keep playing on her mind.

Her mobile chirped, and she lifted it, scanned the screen. *<Maxim will pick you up at 7:30 and will drop you home after your shift. He will do so for the foreseeable future. E xxx>*

One simple text, and yet it reminded her of the good things that were happening in her life. Friends. A sense of building her own opportunities. Making it on her own.

Tucking a strand of hair behind her ear, she glanced at the meals she'd made and packaged during her ruminations. A week's worth of dinners.

She washed up, cleared the counters, and prepared for work.

When the knock came, she was unsurprised.

"Thanks for picking me up, Maxim," she said as she followed him out to his car.

"Not a problem. Ellen said you'd been followed and scared. We have to stick together."

It would be all right. She'd make this work.

Simon lurched around the office. The building transfer had been effected quickly, just as he'd hoped.

The new staff ready to put in place.

Plans drawn up to rehabilitate the building, increase the values. It didn't settle the major issue that gnawed away at him, of course.

Niamh Ryan lived in the building.

Jessica sailed into the office. "Good morning, Simon! The sun is shining, and you've pulled off the purchase of the building. We have a ten o'clock meeting with..." Her words died away after she glanced at his face. "What's wrong?"

He shook his head, but she tsked. Jessica had known him long enough to be aware of every facet of his actions.

"Come on, Simon, spill it."

"It's nothing." The animal within roared its disapproval at the way he brushed off her concerns. *Mate. Protect and adore the mate.* Deep inside him, a struggle for supremacy warred. The human said keep it under wraps, don't let anyone know. The were wanted to lay claim to the only one who'd complete him.

He had to force himself back to the issue. "Where are we at with the work on fencing, security, and how soon will the old super be replaced?"

Jessica's eyebrows shot up. "Well, the fencing shouldn't be an issue. I've got some of our clan on standby to do the job as soon as we decide on the fencing."

He made a "hurry up" motion with his hands, and she blinked.

"Regarding security? Our people are gathering information on what would be best in terms of cameras and locations. Panic buttons, as you requested, and even security on the gate so in order to enter, they need a pass. The old super had a contract, and that's going to be problematic. I've already handed it to our lawyer, and he's looking for an out. Meanwhile, there's been an abduction in the area."

Eight words that nearly stopped his heart beating. "Where?"

"In the park. The young woman was crossing it, we believe late on Monday evening. My sources say she was working late, caught an evening train, and was likely taking a shortcut through the park. They found her handbag and one shoe."

"Who was it?" His hand formed a fist.

Jessica looked down, checked her phone. "A Julia Cummings. Aged twenty-five. Worked for a lycan, Phillip Westerhouse. Do you know him?"

The name didn't ring any bells, but it didn't have to. It wasn't her. Not Niamh Ryan. Still, his instincts told him someone was hunting.

Someone who shouldn't be there.

"I'm contacting my grandfather. I haven't heard from him about someone to track down Julien. The longer we leave it, the colder the trail will get, and we need to find him, shut down his sick little plans."

A niggle set up camp in his brain. He didn't know what or why, just that it was there. He'd let that seed take root and grow, then exploit it.

Jessica nodded. "As soon as I have news on the super issue, I'll let you know. I've got some brochures here too. You need to go through them, choose whichever you think best meets with approval." She slid them onto his desk. "I'm going to get busy with sorting out the insurances and details for where the deposits for the rental fees go. Is there anything else?"

On a whim, he raised his head. "How many tenants do we currently have?"

"Three, but one is planning on moving in the next couple weeks."

He nodded. The single-bedroom apartment Niamh lived in was utilitarian. There were three two-bedroom apartments. He couldn't just move Niamh without it looking odd.

"The remaining tenants, I want them moved into the two-bedroom apartments. No increase in rent. We can redecorate and update the others."

Shock settled on Jessica's face. "No rent increase? Just move them?"

He nodded. If he answered, it might give away the fact that he was interested in her. When the time came to make his advances, he didn't want to do so with a hundred pairs of eyes watching his every move.

"Well, you're the boss. How soon do you want them in the new units?"

"When you can, thanks. Then we can start planning the refurb. I want a fresh coat of paint, check all the carpets and furnishings. Kitchens inspected and whatever needs done, do it."

"Okay," Jessica muttered, shrugging and then retreating.

He turned on the computer and chose the video software, dialled, and waited.

It rang. Rang. Then it disconnected.

"Damn it!" He leaned back in the seat and rubbed his hand over his aching brow. Too many cases of waiting for everyone else and not enough action.

"*M*s Ryan!" The super caught up with her before she could leave the building.

"Yes, Mr Sims?" She smiled, though to be honest, the man was hardly friendly. For the first time, Niamh wondered if it were the case with all supers, just like she'd read, or if only the surly ones caught people's attention?

"Your unit is to be vacated tomorrow."

She sucked in an unsteady breath at the shock of his words. "What?" *Why? What have I done? I'm quiet and tidy. Annoyed no one...*

"You're to be moved to 212. Upstairs. One of the two-bedders."

She blinked. "But I can't afford that!" The words were more of a squeak.

"You're not to be charged any more." He shoved yet another of those endless letters into her hands. "You and 114 are going upstairs. Got informed today along with me being moved on." The wiry man in his sixties grizzled. "Ain't got no respect for a man who's given years of his life..." He turned and walked away from Niamh.

Inside the envelope was a set of keys bearing the tag 212.

A quick look over her shoulder showed her Maxim hadn't yet turned up, so on a whim, she hurried up the stairs, taking care to keep her coat tightly tucked around herself.

On the landing, she scurried along, found the door, and slid the key into the lock.

The lounge was the same size as her entire studio apartment. Off it lay three doors. One was a bathroom with a compact tub, shower and sink. It also had a small machine for washing clothes. "Better than handwashing!" The second room was a child's room with a small single bed, desk, chest of drawers and wardrobe.

The third has to be a bedroom. With a proper bed. It seemed odd that she'd wished for one, and suddenly she had a bigger unit with bedrooms and space! "I don't care. It's mine, and I'm taking the good luck."

Niamh checked her watch and cursed. With a last glance over her shoulder, she headed for the door and went downstairs. She didn't want to keep Maxim waiting any longer than she had to.

He'd just pulled up as she stashed the keys, letter, and phone in her bag. "Thanks for this. It must be a bit of a pain picking me up."

"Nonsense. You and me? We got to stick together. The world is unkind, and nothing comes without a cost."

The words were hard, coming on the heels of her upgraded amenities, and Niamh bit her lip. Was there a catch to her good fortune? Would there be a price to pay?

"You really believe there's a price to pay for everything good that happens?" Inside her, a bright flame of hope danced with fear.

Maxim grunted. "I've been here long enough to see that many things that appear good at the outset simply hide a negative charge until it can't be hidden any longer."

Niamh looked at the fairy, really looked hard, and for the first time noted that the glow most fairies carried about them was dimmed in Maxim. His mouth turned down, and his eyes hazed.

"But if we look at life like that—"

"It's a reality, Niamh. The sooner you embrace it, the sooner you'll be able to come to terms with your future. The only luck to be had is the luck we make ourselves."

Niamh turned to the window, watching as they drove towards the hospital where they worked. She was lost in thought, considering his words, the change in her fortunes, and what may happen next.

CHAPTER 7

*S*imon drove slowly, more than a little aware that today was important. It was the day he'd meet her again. Niamh Ryan. She'd been moved into the better of the two-bedroom apartments and out of the studio she'd inhabited.

He'd not been game to ask his people what her reaction had been, but he hoped it was positive. Opening issues before he was ready to deal with them wasn't the way he worked.

Instead, he'd meet with the marketing people who would advertise the apartments, and hopefully the building would soon be filled. Then he could make a move. He'd get to know Niamh, and he hoped she'd soon understand the value of their connection.

In the darkest recesses of his mind, he was wary. He'd met others who'd been mated, yet their relationship had been unhealthy. Sometimes they didn't work out the way shifters and lycans wanted. In those few cases, the couple only came together long enough to conceive. Then they'd go their separate ways.

And sometimes again, there was more than one who could be the mate of a female. From Simon's perspective, they were special cases. The female and males had to be open to such arrangements before the fates gifted them more than a single mate, to his way of thinking. But that situation wasn't for him. He didn't do so well at sharing.

A vision of Niamh rose in his mind. The human was different somehow from others, and that was why—

He blinked hard, banishing those thoughts. *Concentrate on now.*

Genevieve's mother had been an aberration too; taking two mates in the same heat cycle, her dalliances led to twins. She remained with the first mate because of status, unaware the second child would be a half-breed, or "mutt" as many people unkindly called them. Genevieve had since learned her father was a leprechaun and was coming to terms with that while her soon-to-be husband was now a "turned shifter."

"This world is too complicated to open another can of worms," he muttered.

"What was that, Simon?" Jessica called from the back seat. He'd brought her so she could check the office processes and make adjustments as she saw fit in consultation with the incoming staff.

"Nothing," he growled, castigating himself for speaking out loud.

"You know, talking to yourself won't get you the answers you need," she added, and he grunted.

"I don't need your input there, Jessica." Her peal of laughter poked at the sore spot in his psyche. He knew he talked through issues. It was one of his quirks he'd gotten from his mother, according to Frederick. He didn't remember, having still been quite young when they'd passed.

He drove into the parking lot. They'd painted a spot for "official parking" so when he needed to drop in, he wouldn't have to fight for a spot.

He and Jessica stepped from the car, she with a large briefcase in hand while Simon reached for the box of files and equipment she'd deemed necessary. The new computer system he'd ordered, along with the printer and other accoutrements, had been delivered the day before. She'd set up the office, as they'd agreed, taking over a section of the superintendent's apartment, and she'd arranged the installation of a sliding window.

He glanced up at the building. His people had nearly finished their work in the four weeks he'd taken to prepare for today. Nothing about the process was quick, but he felt that the investment would be worthwhile in the years to come.

Beyond the gates, he noted the long line of people snaking along the sidewalk.

"You've got quite a line-up there," Geoffrey, the new building manager, said as he met Jessica and Simon at the car.

"Yes. At least you should have enough to choose from."

He snorted.

Simon's cell rang. "Simon—"

"I found the investigator finally. Gave him your details, and he said he'll be in touch tomorrow. I haven't been able to track him down until now, as he's been finishing a case." Frederick's voice was thin, as if he'd taken ill.

Simon frowned with worry. "Are you okay, old man?"

Frederick laughed, then broke off with a cough. "Yeah. Bernard brought a cold home, and it's gone through the house. Marta is still down with it, but at least the kids are all over it now."

Huh. Most people thought lycans couldn't catch the common cold. At least in the books. It wasn't quite like that. They got sick, though usually only experiencing mild symptoms unless they were old. That the entire family had struggled... "Does Marta need a healer?"

Frederick laughed. "No. Just another few months."

Simon frowned. "A few...?"

"She's expecting again." If it was possible, Frederick sounded equal parts boastful and terrified.

"That's... that's really quick."

"That's what I said too. But you know how it is. Now I'm just trying to keep her contained and quiet. No easy feat with kids running around everywhere." Frederick sighed. "But we've seen a healer already, and he's going to keep a close eye on her. Once this one comes, we're going to be having a very serious discussion."

Simon could almost imagine them sitting across the table, Marta agreeing with everything until Frederick stopped talking. "Okay, well, when everything settles down, I'll come and visit if that suits."

"Suits? Don't be silly, boy. This is your home, and we're your family. You're always welcome."

"Thanks, Gramps. Look, I have to go now. Take care and stay in touch." They both bid the other goodbye, and Simon closed the connection.

Once the investigation was under way, he could stay in touch with this PI his grandfather had found. Maybe Genevieve would take over responsibility as liaison? She had the skills and experience. Then he could focus on Niamh and building the investments. The pack was growing, and he needed others to step in and take direction of areas he wasn't skilled enough to run.

I'll talk to Jessica about this later, he told himself as he stepped into the newly created office space.

The photocopier in the corner was already doing its duty, printing off the application forms for the prospective tenants, while Jessica unpacked hardbacked clipboards and pens. "At the end of the inspection, we'll get them to fill out these forms that are being copied. We want them placed in the box as they come in. We've got sixty-three known applicants, but there's likely to be some who will drop in too."

He grunted. "So you want me to take them through the building?"

Jessica shook her head. "No. Geoffrey will do that. I'm going to meet them, set them up in groups, and hand out applications. Your job is to peruse them once we've received them. Make sure everything is filled out and start running checks on employers, past building reports, and so on."

The woman before him was not just an efficient manager, she was more like a general on a battlefield lining up the army in readiness of attack. Not for the first time, he was pleased he'd made her his unofficial deputy. When crisis struck—which happened with a monotonous regularity—she'd step up and take control of the day-to-day, releasing him to react.

"When things slow down a bit, you and I are going to talk," he told her.

Jessica winked. "About time you admitted I'm the woman for you." Then she barked a laugh as he rolled his eyes.

It would be simpler for them both, but he looked upon her as a friend. Neither of them would suit for a long-term partner. "No, about making your title official."

Now it was Jessica's turn to freeze. "I... We'll talk later, then."

*N*iamh glanced out the window. In the weeks since she'd moved into the apartment upstairs, there'd been people coming and going. Employees upgrading and painting, repairing and replacing. But nothing like this.

The line snaked down the block for the open inspections that had been advertised widely.

She'd expected to see some people, just not the number that had appeared. Shrugging on a shawl, ensuring her wings were hidden from sight, she opened the front door and stepped out. Emily, from next door, was already there, coffee in hand.

"I never thought I'd see the day when this many people would clamour for a studio apartment."

Niamh smiled uncertainly at the older woman. "I admit I'm a little overwhelmed at the number here. I mean, lots of people we don't know..." Having so many people in the space who were unknown quantities was dangerous. One slip was all it would take, and her secret would be revealed to the world.

She stepped back, ready to retreat, when a presence impinged on her. She turned, and the big man she'd remembered from the inspection climbed up the sheltered stairs to the balcony.

"Good morning, ladies. You may not remember me. My name is Simon." He smiled at them both, and a pit of warmth gathered in Niamh's belly. Interest flared.

"Hi." Emily's eyes twinkled.

"Uh, hello," Niamh muttered, feeling ridiculous standing there simply staring at him.

"Busy day ahead, but I wanted to check in. I would like to talk to you both later about how you've settled in, if you have the time?"

Emily sighed and glanced down at her watch. "I'm afraid I'm going to have to get ready for work. The shop is opening later today, but perhaps some other time?"

Simon agreed as Niamh continued to stand there, frozen to the spot like an ice statue.

"Ms Ryan?"

She jumped. "What? Oh yes. Um, later." *Could I sound any more inane?* "Sorry, I've got a pot on the stove. Making tea." His gaze bored into her, as if seeking something hidden, and she gulped. "I have to go."

"Of course, Ms Ryan. Later today, once we clear the crowds?"

She nodded and retreated behind the door. Closing it firmly, she used it to brace herself because the racing cadence of her heart might yet overwhelm her.

Stupid girl! Careless girl! He's human, and nothing can happen between you.

Reminding herself of those facts didn't stop her heart from wishing.

"*S*eventy-four applications. Thirteen incompletes, so those can be discarded immediately." Jessica smiled. "A significant result. You've made good inroads on checking those applications we can proceed with, and hopefully within a week or two at most, we'll be at full capacity."

Simon was pleased to hear those words. They'd be able to forge ahead, no doubt with a report back to the pack that the initial phase of the investment was a success. But this was merely step one.

His cell beeped once more, just as it had most of the day.

"Simon Bellingham speaking," he answered.

"My name is James Morrow. Your grandfather, Frederick, contacted me to talk to you about a situation you have. I've tied up my latest case and would be happy to talk to you, gain an insight into what you know, what you need, and how I can assist. Does tomorrow at ten thirty at your office suit?"

Simon turned to Jessica. "What's tomorrow looking like? Say ten thirty-ish?"

She slid a diary from her large bag and paged through. "You're free. We have a session with Genevieve and David at three o'clock, but apart from that—"

"I can do ten thirty, James. You have the address of my office?"

"Yes. I make it a rule to learn as much as I can about my clients before I meet with them, Lord of Lycans."

Intrigued, Simon smiled. "Then I'll see you there."

Jessica watched him end the call, a question in her gaze. "Well?"

"Gramps came through with an investigator. He knows who and what we are. Find out what you can about James Morrow." He rattled off the number which had displayed on his cell.

"I'll get what I can by tonight, and then I'm heading off. I've got a date."

Simon stared at her. "A date?"

Jessica smiled gently. "Yes, a date. Set up by the matchmaker, so I can't afford to be late. You know how those women are. Vicious, I tell you. Vicious."

He didn't dare laugh, because having them come after you wasn't something he planned to experience.

With quick moves, Jessica gathered her items. He threw her the keys to the car. "Take it back to my place. I'll catch a cab."

"Oh, sure. Thanks!"

Geoffrey helped her out to the car as Simon watched. Emily hadn't yet returned, and that suited his plans. Geoffrey would return and no doubt soon be busy doing whatever he did.

Now he could go up, using the pretext of updating her on the number of applications for units and how soon they'd fill the building to talk to Niamh. Being near her was like getting up close and personal with a supernova. It heated him up, his soul as much as his body. He craved the heat. The connection. The knowledge that he'd found his one.

Not for the first time, Simon wondered if the cataclysmic meeting was the same for all lycans, or did he feel it more intensely because of who and what he was?

There was a thread of deep and old magic that the lords each carried within themselves. Assuming that mantle wasn't simple or easy. They had to prove their worthiness, undertake the challenges set by the first lords, then consume a meal prepared for them by the keepers of lore—the fairies who lived deep in the forests of the lands they would rule.

He knew they put something in the dish they presented, for he'd felt the welling of power inside him after the first bite of the cinnamon-flavoured vegetable broth that had been given to him that night. No one told him what it was, nor had his grandfather breathed a word about the dreams that followed as he lay under the stars, flashing from man to creature and back again, encircled by a magic fire.

All he knew was in the morning, he'd woken stronger, faster, and ready to assume the mantle of Lord of Lycans.

The clan had gathered, and they'd celebrated for days afterwards while he'd chosen his advisors.

With slow steps, Simon neared Niamh's door. He knocked twice and waited for the door to open.

*N*iamh felt his nearness long before he knocked on the door. She'd prepared as best she could, but hiding wings? Sometimes that was a bigger job than usual. Right then, it teetered on the edge of impossible.

When she let him in, she studied the man. Simon Bellingham wasn't the kind of muscle-bound body builder that seemed to be popular among human women. He was tall—though anyone seemed tall beside her five-foot-four height. His hair was a dirty blond, very similar to hers, and in the depths of his eyes, she could almost see an animal. *Strange.*

She shook her head, willing away the stupidity of that thought.

He was a man, she was a fairy, and any kind of dream she might weave still ended up with them on opposite sides of a chasm too deep to breach.

With that, it was as if a light deep inside sputtered. Was that why Maxim seemed diminished? Was that what he'd experienced?

"Would you like a cup of tea?" Then Niamh realised most Americans preferred coffee. "Or coffee? I have some here, somewhere."

"Tea would be welcome. A reminder of my early years in England."

She blinked. "Oh, so you're not really American, then?"

"Adopted, but my birth country still calls me home from time to time." He settled into a dining chair, watching her bustle around the kitchen. "How do you find the apartment?"

"What? Oh, it's nice. Better than the other. I've got room to move and a proper bed."

The heat of a flush filled her face.

He grinned. "That's good."

She shifted the kettle from the hob, filled the cups and brought them over once she'd disposed of the infusers. "Milk? Sugar? Lemon?"

"Milk, thank you."

She pulled the tiny jug from the refrigerator and set it on the table. He poured some milk into the hot drink, sipped, and set it back down. "Reminds me of my grandma. Before she passed away."

Niamh settled down opposite him. "I'm sorry. You were close?"

Simon nodded, and she watched the play of emotions on his face, the way his jaw pulsed as if he were reliving some intense emotions. "She and my grandfather raised me when my parents and brother died. A long time ago, though."

Without thinking, she reached out, placed her hand over his, and squeezed. "Those who pass beyond are never far from us."

He cocked his head. "A wise comment I've heard more than once."

Niamh swallowed. Those were the words of commendation on

the passing of lycans and fairies. She'd better watch herself, lest she give something away she shouldn't.

She sipped her tea while every nerve danced at his nearness.

"What do you do for work, Ms Ryan?"

Coughing on her drink, Niamh struggled for oxygen. "I... work... at the hospital... as a domestic assistant."

"And do you enjoy it?"

She shook her head. "I wanted to study healing and medicine, but there was no money."

He frowned. "No one would help you, Niamh?"

His use of her name in that liquid tongue melted her knees, along with other parts of her anatomy.

"Large family, Mr Bellingham. Mouths to feed, so I came out here, in the time-honoured tradition of your adopted country, to make my own way."

"Simon," he corrected her, and she swallowed.

"Mr Bellingham, I don't see how any of this impacts the apartment."

"It doesn't, Niamh. But I met you, and at that moment, my life changed. I changed. I want to get to know you better."

Those dratted nerves attacked her, and she tugged her hand away. "I don't have time for a boyfriend, Simon. Besides, it would be unwise."

"Why?" He leaned in, that mesmerising fire in his eyes growing hotter.

"Because..." she answered, more than a little aware of how weak that single word sounded.

"I don't believe you're afraid of me, Niamh."

Anger flashed through her. "I'm not! But humans are—" She clapped her hand over her mouth, regretting that one word that slipped out.

"What would you know of paranormals, Niamh?" His brow furrowed. "Apart from vampires. You know more. Otherwise, you wouldn't have chosen that term."

She blanched. "Please don't press me. I can't talk about it."

He thrust away from the table and made a slow circle of the lounge, this time really looking, taking it all in.

The circlet hung on the wall. The tokens of memory…

He touched one and turned back to her. "Fairy. You're a fairy?"

Oh no! This can't be happening! I didn't give it away, please!

His smile grew larger, reminiscent of a dog gaining a treat. "Excellent. Then I don't have to hide my nature. Hi, my name is Simon Bellingham, and I'm the Lord of Lycans."

She fainted.

*S*imon cursed as she hit the ground with a thud. He slid his hands beneath her folded body and raised her up, moving through to the lounge and laying her on the couch.

It wasn't enough that he'd pushed her so hard that she'd made the disclosure. He knew fairies were odd with keeping their secrets. Retribution in the wrong circumstances could be deadly to them. He regretted that now, glancing down at her pale visage.

That he'd been drawn to her was a surprise. He was an alpha, while fairies were the equivalent of the nerds of the paranormal world.

Or more like oil and water, his mind added.

That she'd reacted as she did? It hit him hard, just like a body blow might. Stole his breath, and for a moment he could almost feel the rictus of pain radiating through his body.

Breathe in. Breathe out. Release the negative emotions into the heavens.

He'd learned that mantra while still young. It wasn't perfect, but it helped him to find a calmer centre.

As the adrenaline wore off, he glanced back at her. Such a slight woman. Curved gently in all the right places. He'd have to be careful with her once they were together in the fullest sense of the word. Weres were known for their power and stamina.

He'd rip out his heart long before he hurt her.

Her eyes fluttered open. "What… what happened?"

He moved to her side, crouched down, and took her hand. "I pushed you too hard, Niamh. You fainted."

She blushed, and her gaze skittered away. "I'm so sorry, my lord. I didn't realise—"

He brushed away a lock of hair. "You wouldn't. You haven't been here long enough, I dare say, to make the connections among my own. We keep to ourselves and don't live out in the open. Well, most of us don't, anyway."

Her eyes flicked to him. "I should have known, read the energy, but I've been busy, working..."

Simon sighed. "I can imagine. Your job would entail long hours. But it's not what you want?"

"One day, when I'm more established, I intend to study. To become a healer. My token is a dragonfly."

He smiled, aware that was a powerful totem of her kind. "Change. Growth. That makes sense. But where is your family? I hear the lilt of Ireland in your voice."

Niamh groaned. "I was sent here, a banishment of sorts. I need to find my own way, to prove myself before I can return home."

Odd. Why on earth had they banished her? She was obviously young and untouched. Fairies had many rules, it was true, but how might she have transgressed to earn this sentence? His mind told him not to push harder. He held his tongue.

"Perhaps you know the fairies of the glades around here? Ellen, my sponsor, says she has no contact, and neither does Maxim."

In his chest, the hidden wolf raised its head. Maxim. A man's name. Why did another man figure so highly in her life, and how? "Maxim?" It took every ounce of willpower to control himself.

"He works with Ellen and me. Picks me up for work and—" Niamh bolted upright. "Ohmygosh! Work." She glanced at the clock and groaned. "He'll be here soon. It's nearly five, and I need to change and—"

He rose, offering her a hand. "Are you sure you're able? I mean, you fainted."

Her smile was thin. "I can't take time off. Not right now. I need to make it through my trial period, and I'm due to meet with the supervisor tomorrow. He'll check my work, so I have to go." She spoke firmly, as if telling herself it would all be fine.

Simon didn't like that. She was too slight and small to be undertaking such onerous work, but right now, he couldn't quite claim her, so he gritted his teeth. "Then I guess I should leave."

Niamh nodded. "I need to shower and eat and... you know."

"When do you have a day off?"

With a blink, she stared at him. "Why?"

"Because I'd like to get to know you."

Simon watched as surprise skittered across her face. "I... uh, day after tomorrow."

"Then I'll be here around four to collect you. I don't suppose you've gone out of town, have you? There's some private green space that belongs to my grandfather. We can be there in under an hour."

Her mouth dropped open. "Why would you do that?"

Tamping down on the answer he wanted to give was like caging a cloud. "Because you probably need time to refresh in the green."

"I... That's very kind, but—"

"Good. Then be ready." He turned to leave, but at the door, he stopped and looked over his shoulder. "Bring your circlet," he added with a smile, then shut the door on her surprised expression.

*S*imon waited in his office for James Morrow to arrive. He did. Promptly. His car was a nondescript black SUV. He parked it with the minimum of fanfare, and at ten thirty, he knocked on the door.

Simon watched it all from the CCTV mounted on the wall, streaming to his computer.

He didn't look like any kind of normal investigator Simon had worked with previously. His suit was immaculately tailored, fitting like the proverbial glove. His dark hair was artfully cut, so it looked like a waterfall that fell just below his chin. Grey eyes, piercing in their intensity. For a moment, Simon wondered about who and where he came from, then dismissed the thought. *So long as he can do the job.*

The man waltzed in and took a seat opposite Simon. "Frederick told me you have a situation. One that might be tricky."

The scent of vampire and something else filled Simon's awareness, and he blinked. "Correct. There's a pack from the southern region. It didn't affiliate to us. However, one youngster—the son of the beta—has gone rogue. He's attacked those nested with unhoused vampires. Killed humans. We have to find him and bring him to justice. He poses a threat to two members of my clan, both recent additions. One was the *Yeux Secondes* of a local house."

"Indeed. A were who was previously the human second eye of a vampire master. That would have to be David, yes?"

Simon tapped a hand on the top of his desk. "You seem well informed."

"I make it my job to know about my clients. I know Frederick is your grandfather. Your parents are both dead. I also know David is associated with three of the local nests. One of the masters is the life partner of his sister, Hope. His cousins, Celina and Daniel, are also life partnered to highly ranked vampires, and in particular Cressida. I'm intrigued by this situation. Tell me more about this case." James steepled his hands and settled back in the chair.

Simon told him about Julien—Genevieve's previous lover—and the threats he'd made. He talked of how the nests couldn't directly involve themselves in the investigation, as the fallout from capturing Attar had stretched their capacity.

"I'll take it on, on one condition."

Simon quirked a brow.

"I want an introduction to Cressida."

"I'm not sure I can—"

James waved a hand. "She won't know my name and won't take a call from me, but I have information that would be worthwhile to the nests. It's information that may answer some questions she has. It will save lives."

Simon considered the request. As far as payments went, it wasn't onerous.

"Fine. I'll contact Cressida, tell her you wish to meet. But more than that, I can't promise."

James smiled. "That's enough for now."

CHAPTER 8

*N*iamh got through the next few days suffering highs and lows.

"Now, Ms Ryan, thank you for joining me. I'm pleased to advise the hospital plans to formalise your employment with us. Your work has been exemplary, and you've only been late once with a notation from your supervisor that it was because of an incident on your way to work. While we can't condone any form of unofficial absenteeism, you made contact immediately, and we're prepared to overlook this anomaly so long as this is the only time."

Mr Garrut smiled, an oily obsequious grin that left a grimy feeling in Niamh's gut.

"As to the shift you're working, we have seen fit to change you to the day shift. We need a reliable worker, and—"

Niamh's breath caught in her throat. "But, Mr Garrut, as Ellen has explained, I have a medical condition that—"

"And we're willing to overlook that, Ms Ryan. The change of shift will become effective from next Thursday. Now, if that's all?" It wasn't really a question, and in the depths of his eyes, she read satisfaction that he'd achieved his own ends. She might want and need to argue, but her position was still precarious. No one could know why she couldn't work during the day when there were so many others around.

She bit her lip, contained the tears of terror, and rose with a nod, accepting the envelope he handed to her. No doubt it contained all the information he'd just dropped on her.

Exiting the office, she bumped into Ellen. "Well?"

"The job is mine, but, Ellen, they're changing me to the day shift. What do I do?"

Ellen's eyes popped. "What? No, that can't be right."

She worked long and tiring hours at the hospital. By the time her day off came, she dropped onto the bed into a deep and dreamless sleep. The fear that Ellen wouldn't be able to argue against the change of shift had been compounded by the number of people moving into the complex, the quiet of the previous status quo having been overlaid with people coming and going. More people meant the greater the chance she'd be seen.

Her gut tied in knots, and food wasn't welcome with the level of upset she experienced over this decision.

When she woke, she felt wrung out, terrified about what was going to happen, and going out with Simon—*Lord of Lycans*, she firmly reminded herself—really wasn't ranking highly in the pleasurable stakes.

He commanded weres, had now requested her presence. She'd honour the tradition of "walking beside them along the earth softly" and prepare.

"I won't wear my flower gown," she told herself, instead choosing a light sundress, which she paired with a deceptively lightweight cardigan. It would hide her wings, but she could divest herself of it once they reached the woodlands. She placed her circlet into a small muslin bag and slid it into the backpack she'd carry.

She simply brushed her hair until it shone. Then Niamh settled in to wait for him.

At four on the dot came the rap, firm and manly. *Just like him.*

Without considering, she swung the bag over her shoulder and answered the door. He was dressed in casual jeans and a polo that moulded to his physique.

Her mouth dried.

"Come with me, Niamh," he said, eyes wolfish as he held out his hand to her.

She took it, knowing hers trembled with the strength of emotions she wished she could suppress. Lust wasn't an unknown quantity to her. Many fairies partook of sexual experiences, treating them as a necessity of life. She hadn't. Something had told her to wait. So she had. Trusting her innermost intuition had seen her through life. Well, mostly.

You didn't see your banishment coming, did you?

"No, I didn't," she muttered.

"Everything all right, Niamh?" His voice broke through her introspection, and she jumped.

"What? Oh yes. Just thinking out loud."

He led her down to a hulking tank of a car, and she read the badge. Oh yes, very masculine and point making. Suited to the alpha.

She climbed in once he opened the door, settling herself while he made his way around to the other side. "Seat belt?"

She blinked. "Oh yes." She fastened it on herself.

He started the car, and she realised he was silent. Would he think it odd? Her rude?

Once they were moving away from town, he cleared his throat. "Something's bothering you. You're distracted."

"Just work things," she said, hoping he'd leave the subject alone.

"Anything I can do to assist?"

Niamh turned towards him. "Not unless you have pull with the hospital's HR division. They're changing my shift. To daytime."

When his brow furrowed with confusion, she sighed.

"I work at night because there's so few people around. I'm less likely to be exposed, but I finished my trial and they put me on full time, on the understanding that I'd work night shifts only on account of a 'medical issue.'" She made the air quotes and glanced at the passing scenery. "Lots more people and a greater chance I'll be found out. Ellen, my supervisor, has been trying to get them to change their minds, but they're adamant. So unless I can find another job, I'm stuck with days."

That reality scared the living daylights out of her. She'd grown up listening to the cautionary tales of fairies discovered and what happened to them. Times might have been more enlightened now, and vampires were openly walking around, but fairies continued to maintain their anonymity because they were weaker, not fighters or warriors, and couldn't protect their own.

"Would you prefer to work elsewhere?" he asked.

"Yes, I wish I could work somewhere else. I'd take just about anything in a heartbeat."

He reached out, placed a hand on hers. "You're really terrified, aren't you, Niamh?"

She nodded as tears pricked her eyes. "But I don't know what else I can do or even how. Ellen arranged my green card when Mam told me I was to leave home."

"Why was that?"

She curled into herself. "Please, I'm not sure I can talk about it."

He rubbed his thumb over her knuckles. "Okay, perhaps someday you'll tell me, when you're ready. How soon do you have to start the new shifts?"

"Thursday."

He grunted. "I know people. Leave it with me, and I'll see what can be done."

Niamh whirled in her seat. "I... You don't have to. I know I'm not your responsibility."

"I do it because I care, Niamh. Let me see what I can do, okay?"

The pressure in her chest lifted a little, and she sank back into the seat. "Thank you, my lord."

"Simon," he corrected.

"But you're—"

"Simon."

She smiled a little at the ferocity in his voice. "All right, then, Simon."

CHAPTER 9

Another day and another girl. This one was tiny and red-headed. There was a fae quality about her. She didn't smell like magic, but she moved as if nothing could touch her. That was enough for him.

His prey danced eagerly along the footpath in the gloom.

The game he'd been playing had to change, because it no longer gave him the same thrill.

So tonight, he'd watch and follow, gather information and find a fresh way to fill the hunger that carved his insides hollow.

Tomorrow night, he'd strike. Take her from her safe place. Play and celebrate his new achievement.

Gorge himself when the time came.

"A very fulfilling plan," he muttered, jumping to another vantage point, while the bag over his shoulder swung against him. He stilled the motion absently.

And if he found someone else during that time, for a longer game again, then so much more to his fulfillment.

He sighed and dropped the sack to the rooftop. No one ever came here. They'd never found the others. He smirked at the rows, carefully hidden away where only he could see. He dragged the sack over, stashed it beside the last.

"Sleep well, my love."

Then he whirled and moved, a shadow in the gloom as he followed the girl to her home. He watched from beneath an oak and smiled. "Tomorrow, my love. Tomorrow."

CHAPTER 10

 imon watched the smile on her face, the way her entire body relaxed the minute she set foot on the green grass beneath the leafy trees.

When Niamh donned her circlet and removed the grey cardigan, releasing her wings, her laugh tinkled around him. The trees returned the sound, shaking their leaves, while a bevy of dragonflies came from nowhere.

"Simon, do you see them?" She whirled and danced, her wings beating fast in a blur, and all he could think was how beautiful she was. How in tune with nature.

Her wings were iridescent in the sunlight. As she rose, they beat and caught the light, a rainbow shimmering.

Breathtaking.

A sound pealed around them, like the twinkling of a million wind chimes, all in perfect harmony and he turned as other fairies entered the glade.

Niamh flew to the ground and moved near to him as if she expected some kind of punishment.

"Niamh?"

"I must be formally invited. This is their glade."

He cleared his voice as the oldest female glided towards them both. "Lord of Lycans, this is an honour. You've brought a friend."

Niamh dipped into a low curtsey. "I am Niamh Ryan. I seek only to refresh, not to intrude, lady."

The woman who'd spoken smiled. "And you are welcome, child. I am Kaiah, and I am the glade guardian." She touched Niamh's face gently, and Niamh's expression of wonderment nearly broke Simon's heart. "You are welcome here, dear. A friend of the Lord of Lycans is always an acceptable guest."

The others gathered around and introduced themselves. This wasn't the place where he'd come into his powers, but they read the power he exuded, having taken pains to ensure he at least had cordial interaction with as many herds of fairies as possible.

Niamh smiled with pleasure, the light she exuded somehow sparkling with green, red, and gold. Her wings beat furiously as she rose with a joyous laugh.

"You honour us with your presence, Lord. Tell me, what are your intentions towards Niamh?" The words were gentle, but he read the concern in Kaiah's tone.

"She is my mate."

Kaiah's brow rose. "That is... unusual."

"Indeed. I have not yet broached it with her, but the connection is there. Strong."

"She is afraid she will be rebuked, I fear."

Simon grunted. "She was banished from her homeland. Sent here to find her own way."

Kaiah sighed, the sound heavy with understanding. "Many of the old-world country fairies do that when there is a difficulty. They break the faith or the rules, but I doubt she is the latter, being so innocent."

When he looked at her, brow raised to find out why, Kaiah laughed. "She wears a veil of innocence around her. She has no supports?"

"Her supervisor, Ellen, and the male she travels with to and from work. I believe both are fairies."

Kaiah looked aghast. "Three fairies without support? How can this be?"

That was a question Simon couldn't answer, so he shrugged.

"A welcome must be extended." She beckoned to another fairy and whispered something in his ear. He flitted away, returning moments later with two white feathers wrapped in yellow bows. "Please ask Niamh to give these to her friends. They will be welcome here."

He may not exactly understand the symbolism, but there was no doubt in his mind as to their sincerity.

"I will."

She led him to a circle in the middle of the glade. "Come, drink with us. Niamh?" she called. "Will you join us?"

Niamh hovered just above the ground. "It will be my pleasure, lady."

Kaiah smiled, and the rest of the fairies settled down as small cups appeared along with a teapot. He knew better than to ask where they'd come from, as fairy magic was connected to the earth.

The tea was spicy and refreshing, and he sipped it. When they were done, he rose. "We should leave now. Thank you for allowing us to enter and enjoy this beautiful place."

"Well, don't be a stranger, then. Bring Niamh and her friends to visit again soon."

As they retreated, Simon considered the questions that were unanswered and the information Kaiah had shared.

"She was very kind, the lady Kaiah. In face the entire herd was. We're invited back to celebrate high summer and winter. These are most important festivals." Niamh practically bubbled over with excitement and enthusiasm, her wings once more tucked into the grey cardigan and the circlet in her bag.

He almost mourned the change, but her face continued to shine for the rest of the trip back to town.

When his cell rang in the car, he excused himself to take the call.

"Simon speaking."

"James Morrow. We have a problem."

He grunted and wanted to ask the man to ring back, but his job was to lead the pack, so instead he asked, "What?"

"Julien has not been seen leaving the city. His new car is parked at an apartment building in Mohawk Valley. Near your apartment building."

A lump lodged in Simon's throat. "Whereabouts?"

James gave an address, and Simon's gut plummeted. Mere streets away from where Niamh was living.

"It gets worse. There's been at least three abductions in the last few weeks of women walking in the night. One worked for a paranormal. The other had dated one previously, though it wasn't widely known. There was another last night."

Niamh's face paled, and Simon reached out, placing a hand on hers. "What do you need?"

James tsked down the line. "I need time and resources. I'll send you some information, but you have apartments near there. Can you make one available to me?"

"Leave it with me," he growled. "I'll be in touch later today." They'd made all the placements, but Niamh lived there. Perhaps he could talk her into relocating. But where?

His mind whirled. She would argue about staying with him. Where else? He could ask Jessica, since she lived alone. Perhaps she might make her spare room available while Simon wooed Niamh and got her safely away from the newly discovered danger zone?

He turned to look at Niamh. "A slight change of plans. I have to head to my home for something. Come with me?"

She bit her lip. The fullness of those luscious plump pillows worried by her teeth had him responding with a groan. "Niamh, I'm a man."

She blinked at him. "What?"

"You're a beautiful woman. One I'm personally interested in."

Her mouth formed an *O* of surprise. "But I'm very ordinary. Really, I am. Nothing special, Simon."

He wanted to belt the person who'd made her think there was

nothing about her that might drive a man wild. "Trust me, Niamh. Nothing about you is ordinary or dull."

Her cheeks took on a pale pink hue. Her blush was delightful. "You mustn't say that, Simon. Please."

He wished he could stop the car, take her chin in his hand, and show her just how intriguing she was. And how much he wished he could do more. But she wasn't ready, and they were on a major road. Instead he growled, "I would show you what I mean, but not yet. You're not ready, and right here isn't the place."

He drove in silence, the air in the car close and full of hunger.

Once he made it to his house, he invited her inside. She trailed him, footsteps slow and uncertain.

He glanced at the unassuming house from her perspective. It was small, though not tiny. The traditional Victorian house was painted grey and white, but the gardens were filled with pretty flowers, the aesthetic welcoming to the eye.

Her breath caught. "It's beautiful."

"I like it. It's not huge, but it meets my needs. Jessica, my business manager, tells me that if I wasn't using a section of the downstairs for office space, it would be completely wasted on me."

"Oh no," Niamh whispered. "It's welcoming and warm. Just like..." She blushed again, and this time, he couldn't help himself as he dragged her close.

"What?"

"It's like you." She ducked her head, and this time, he didn't stop his instinctive reaction. He slid his hand to her chin and raised it so their gazes met. As his mouth lowered to hers, he watched the dilation of her pupils, heard the sigh that escaped her lips.

He kissed her. *Such a tame word*, his mind declared at the pleasure of the contact. Her mouth stilled as his lips connected with hers.

"Kiss me back," he muttered.

She pulled back. "I don't..." Her eyes were glazed. "I don't know how," she whispered, and the animal roared within in.

Kaiah had been right to call her an innocent, he thought, cupping her soft cheek with a sigh. "I'll have to teach you, then, won't I?"

But she'd retreated already, emotionally and physically. He wanted to growl with frustration but contained it. He wouldn't scare her. Not for the entire world.

*N*iamh might never have experienced sexual hunger, but she wasn't unaware of it. She'd seen the pairings among friends and family, but never had she wanted to participate in the earthy activities. Not until now.

Simon. Lord of Lycans. There was a zing about him that made her want to bask in his proximity. She wanted to learn how to kiss him, to please him. Wanted the pleasure, she was sure he would bring her.

She followed him into the house. It was indeed beautiful. Tastefully decorated inside and out, she thought. The flowers in the front attracted all kinds of insect life, and she was sure dragonflies might also flit in the garden, which was a delightful riot of colour.

He pulled her into his office—at least she guessed that was what it was as she wandered around looking at the photos that covered the bookcases. Pictures of a couple, where the man appeared to be in his fifties with a woman a little younger, and three children sitting on their laps. More pictures of them with another child with round, chubby baby cheeks. An older photo sat beside it of a couple and two children. The man looked similar to Simon, and she wondered if they were his parents.

He had taken up location at his desk, looking every inch the entrepreneur as he murmured into his phone, booting up his computer and rifling through files.

The books on his shelves were just as intriguing: *Helfcotte's Law of Lycan*, *Lycanthropy: Myth and Legend*, and *Lycans: A Misunderstood Tribe*. There were also the latest blockbuster tales by authors she'd heard of, along with business tomes.

On the wall hung several certificates, including a bachelor's degree and a master's as well.

She turned to look at him, then squeaked with surprise to find him hovering at her shoulder.

"Find anything interesting?" he murmured.

"Um..." Unable to answer, she skirted around him and moved into a guest chair, clasped her hands, and prepared to wait, willing herself to fall into a light meditation. Anything rather than face the fact that his nearness was intoxicating.

He sank down beside the seat. "What do you want to do next, Niamh?"

What a coward you are!

Opening her eyes, she took in the sapphire orbs before her. "I don't know, Simon." Her words were a whisper, and there was a power that drew her closer. The tang of his breath whispered over her lip, and she shivered.

"Niamh..." His voice dropped in timbre and he gripped her shoulder, drew her closer. "Is this what you want?"

Do I ever! "I... I do, but I'm frightened, Simon. There are feelings I don't understand to untangle. I mean, I know about intimacy, the physical union, but these feelings..." She turned away, embarrassed to be telling him these truths.

"Never be ashamed that you want me, Niamh. I want you too."

Those words sent sparks racing through her body.

"You're not ready. I won't push you, Niamh, but I want something with you. A relationship, not just sex."

Niamh swallowed. "But how will I know?"

He brushed a lock of hair from her face. "You'll know. When the time is right. But come, I'll show you the house. The backyard."

She took his hand, sure there was a deeper meaning but also scared to lose the connection between them.

They walked through the house, and he told her the history of it as she listened intently. Not just to the words but the cadence that betrayed his affection for the place.

They'd just headed to the back when a woman appeared.

"Jessica. Come meet Niamh. She's a..." He paused for a fraction of a second. "A friend. She's wanting to enrol in healing—"

Niamh watched the blond-haired, blue-eyed woman who strolled across the patio as if she owned it. *Is that jealousy?* The snarky thought was unknown and very unwelcome.

"Really? Wow! Dr Arnett is looking for a paid intern. Someone who wants to be involved in shifter health studies long term."

"Oh. I didn't know that," Simon said.

Jessica smiled. "She's just announced it, and you know the difficulties she had last time. If Niamh has a résumé, I'd be more than happy to put it forward to her."

Niamh's gut twisted. This woman she'd just felt nasty thoughts of wanted to help her?

"I... I do," she murmured. "I can email it from home."

"Sure thing. Email it to Simon, and he'll make sure I get it. Simon's a great boss and an awesome pick of people, if he's willing to vouch for you?"

Simon smiled. "Absolutely."

He doesn't even know me! Niamh opened her mouth to remonstrate, but he flicked the end of her nose.

"But she'll need alternative accommodation too. She doesn't drive and—"

Jessica grimaced. "I would help, but I've recently found someone..."

Simon frowned. "Oh." He rubbed his brow with a finger.

"But you've got rooms here. Why doesn't Niamh rent one from you?"

Shock stole Niamh's breath, but Simon smiled. "Do you think that would be appropriate?"

Jessica appeared to appraise him silently. "I think you'd be making the best use of resources. Dr Arnett's office is only just down the road. She could walk. Besides, you need someone else rattling around in this cavernous place. It's a win-win situation as far as I can tell."

CHAPTER 11

*S*imon waited for an hour after returning home from dropping Niamh off, his laptop open on his desk. A ding sounded, and he checked the email. Niamh Ryan's résumé was attached, and he smiled.

The gods were smiling on him at this point. He clicked Send on the email to Dr Arnett and sat back, wondering how soon he'd receive a reply.

Thank you for emailing Edina Arnett. I will respond as soon as I can; however, please be aware that lengthy waits may apply.

"I hope to hell not." The sooner he could find Niamh alternative employment more suited to her obvious interest and bring her home to live, the sooner he could sort the next issue out. James Morrow required a place to stay so he could be "on the spot" dealing with the Julien issue.

An article entered his inbox, and he opened it.

Missing woman Julia Cummings's handbag and shoes were retrieved in an alley this evening. The situation has not been resolved, and police fear foul play is involved.

In the back of his mind, Simon wondered if there was some connection to the Julien situation. If that was the case, then having Niamh here, safely under his roof, made sense.

An email dinged, and he turned off the news article to see a reply from Edina Arnett.

Simon, thanks for sending the résumé through. If you're happy to vouch, we could try a trial, perhaps. Do you know how soon she may be available?

Unwilling to take anything for granted, he rang Niamh, connecting to her voicemail. He left a message and sat back in his chair, wondering not for the first time at the speed with which his life had changed.

The depths of the emotions he was experiencing were a surprise. He didn't know quite what he should have expected, but not this primal need to ensure her safety, to be near her and assist her with finding something more attuned to her skills and interests.

His phone pealed, and he glanced down to read Niamh's text.

<As soon as it's offered, I guess. I can give my notice at any time.>

Not one to wait, he raised the phone to his ear and called Dr Arnett. "I've just spoken with Niamh, and as soon as you need her, she can be available."

A quickly indrawn breath met his announcement. "Really? That's amazing. I wonder if she'd be willing to start on Monday. That way she could shadow Lisa until her last day in four weeks."

"I'll ring her and let her know."

"Simon, I can't thank you enough. After the issues I had finding Lisa, I was dreading the recruitment process."

As soon as he hung up from Edina, he dialled Niamh. "So, get ready to hand in your notice. Your new job starts Monday." Silence followed. "Niamh?"

"I can't believe it. Thank you, Simon. I feel like a lifelong dream is finally coming true." Her voice cracked on the last word.

"So, when do I pick you up to move you in?"

Silence stretched once again. "I'm not sure that's so wise."

Rolling his eyes with frustration, he bit back the growl that wanted to rise in his throat. *Protect your mate,* his inner animal urged. If she'd been here beside him, he probably could have kissed her, scattered her wits, and talked her into it. "I'd feel better having you here. Knowing where you were." He had to walk a fine line. Nothing had been assured yet.

"Give me a week or two. Let me prove I can do the job first. Then if you need..." Sounds rose and then muffled as if she'd laid a hand over the phone. "Look, I have to go. I'll... I'll call you in the morning, when I finish my shift."

It wasn't nearly enough, but for now, he had to be satisfied.

Even as he readied for bed later on, he still felt a ripple of concern. Why, he couldn't say. After all, she'd been safe enough for the last three months. What difference would a couple weeks make?

*A*s Niamh let herself in the security gates, an itch began at the nape of her neck. She turned, scanned the darkened streets. Nothing and no one. She waved off Maxim, who pulled away from the kerb and trudged towards the steps.

A sound had her whirling, blood pulsing rapidly in her throat.

Just your imagination.

A door beside the steps opened, and Niamh glanced up. Bailey, a big muscular man, filled the doorway. "Niamh, you're home. Good. I'll wait until you're upstairs and inside."

Since Bailey, Damien, and Ulrich had taken on the role of combined superintendents and security, she felt so safe. Protected.

She knew they worked for Simon but didn't question that one or another of them was always awake and waiting for her. "Thanks, Bailey. I'm going straight to bed."

The man smiled, and she made her weary way up the steps, feeling as if she'd fall flat on her face. She'd handed in her notice immediately, on Ellen's suggestion. That way she had a few days to re-acclimate to day work and time to find clothes appropriate to her new role. Maxim would pick up the mucky grey-blue uniforms tomorrow evening.

Reaching the safety of her door, she glanced down the steps to see Bailey patiently waiting for her to go inside. She almost did when a sound caught her attention, hair raising as she glanced up to see someone—or something—on top of the building opposite.

She must have squeaked because in an instant, Bailey was up the steps. "What's wrong?"

"There's someone over there." She pointed to the building, but upon glancing from Bailey to the grey brick structure, it was gone.

He sniffed the air, much like a dog would. "I... Get inside, Niamh. I'll get Ulrich to check it out."

She did so, shooting the deadbolt to be sure, but she hovered near the door. The tempo of her heartbeat rose, nerves jangling and dancing below the surface of her skin.

Time passed. Minutes or hours, she couldn't say, though it dragged and she still waited.

Two sharp raps on her door had her jumping, and Niamh cautiously glanced through the peephole, only exhaling and reaching for the locks when Bailey's face came into view.

He urged her forwards and locked the door behind him. "I've already contacted Simon. He's on his way. Grab your clothes and stuff. Do you need help?"

Something in his harried tone ratcheted up her terror. "What's going on?"

"There was someone there. Ulrich is contacting the police, but we need you out of here. Protecting your anonymity is important. Simon was most clear about that. As far as the police will be aware, I was undertaking my regular patrols. Now come on. Pack. Quickly. Whatever we can't fit straight away can be sent on after."

Bailey pushed her forwards, and this time, Niamh didn't argue. "Grab my laptop and the small bag on the lounge. I'll gather my clothes and—"

"I'll get your toiletries too. Is there anything in the kitchen?"

She shook her head, urgency beating in her blood. Her suitcase lay in the lounge. She whipped around, picking up her memory tokens and the few photos she'd finally set out. With the circlet deposited in the box's top, Bailey grabbed her bag and led her down the stairs and into the office just as the flashing lights of the police car pulled up across the road.

"There's a back door," Bailey explained. "Simon will be here in a few minutes, and we'll get you out through it."

Sure enough, he was there in well under ten minutes. The concern on Bailey's face smoothed out once she, the box, and her suitcase were safely deposited in the car and they drove into the night.

"Are you all right?" Simon's hand slid over hers.

"I... Yes. I mean, I know little about—"

"I'll explain later." He grunted and pressed the phone button. Bailey's name flashed on the dash. "Thanks for that. When they're finished, I want to meet with you and Ulrich at my office."

"Simon, you know we wouldn't let anything happen to her. The danger was obvious. But we'll give you a full accounting once the police are cleared. Ulrich said you'd probably want Genevieve in on it too."

She watched as Simon's brow rose. "Okay, I'll make contact once she's settled."

Niamh didn't like feeling like a package. "What's the problem, Simon?" she asked as soon as he disconnected.

He glanced in her direction. "I'm not sure you really want to know."

"I'm not some precious little snowflake, you know. Tell me."

He glanced at her. "When we get home."

She opened her mouth to argue, but he shook his head.

"Please. Just trust me."

She crossed her arms and fumed the rest of the way to his house.

CHAPTER 12

He snarled.

This was not the way he wanted it to go. The girl who'd eluded him before was hiding in the apartments opposite and, by the smell of it, consorting with weres.

His lips parted in a wide smile before he remembered what he'd lost with a single incautious move. She'd seen him, as had that burly were watching her. Now he'd lost all his trophies. Every single one.

"Bastards."

They'd pay. They'd have to.

He looked to the little birdie he still held in a cage. Her time had come. Staying in this location wasn't any good. They might come upon him while he played.

He raised the cell to his ear. "Julien, we have a problem."

"We always do when you're left alone. What?"

"I was made tonight. By one of my targets. My home has been compromised. I need another."

A hiss echoed on the line. "You need me to line up another lair?"

He winced at Julien's chosen term. He'd never before considered it a lair; it was a home and a play centre all rolled into one, but he hadn't told Julien that he used this building for that, only for his recycling and dumping ground. But perhaps he might gain some further equipment because of this hiccup. That would be a silver lining, and he supposed he could live with the choice of word. Maybe even embrace it.

"I need somewhere new. Clean. I need a cage, and I'll have to replace my equipment."

Julien was silent for a moment. "I'll see what can be arranged. We'll have to use a different house. Can't have anyone tagging us, can we? By the way, I have a pickup for you, once you're ready."

He smiled. "Of course. Be happy to."

CHAPTER 13

Simon knew Niamh was downright furious with him. Hell, he likely would be too, but everything he'd done was to keep her safe. Not that she knew it yet. He'd have to confess, though, once Bailey and Ulrich turned up. Meanwhile, he'd settled her in the guest room and attempted to dive into work.

Morrow would move into the apartment tomorrow once he'd arranged for the last of Niamh's things to be removed.

He had to contact Genevieve, and the day-to-day decisions of the pack were no easy feat to accomplish. He had squabbles between two neighbouring clans to adjudicate, and three youngsters needed to be sentenced to community service for worrying a farmer's cows. 'Just for fun,' as they'd termed it.

Jessica waltzed in. "So, I see there's a box in the hallway. I figure that means Niamh is here, and she's starting soon with Dr Arnett, yes?"

He growled, and she came closer.

"Someone was out there. Watching her. Bailey and Ulrich will be in later to report. I left a message on Genevieve's cell that we need her here for that, and I'd like you in on it too. We've got a Council meeting tomorrow, and I plan to put forward your nomination for 2IC."

Jessica started. "What? What the ever-loving hell have you been snorting, Simon? There's never been a female beta of any pack."

He grinned, letting her words wash over him. "True. But there's always a first, you know."

Her eyes glinted. "What if I said I don't want the responsibility?"

This time he chuckled. "You not want responsibility? You, who fought out five men for the position of my office manager?"

She grimaced. "But why would you do that? A beta is usually chosen only if the alpha is aging." She slumped into the chair opposite him.

"Times have changed, Jess. We've got so many damn responsibilities, and things change rapidly. I need someone I can rely on to make decisions on the run. Someone I can trust."

"Well..." She clenched her hands together. "I guess that makes us a formidable team, then, doesn't it? You, me, and Niamh."

"Something like that. About Niamh. She's... Someone was watching her from the building opposite the apartments. Bailey came out to check, and she took fright. He got her inside the building."

"And does Niamh know you placed people in the building there to keep her safe? To monitor her?"

The blush built from his chest, a burning tide. "No. I didn't want her to know, but—"

Jess glared at him. "In the spirit of sisterhood, I have to tell you you're digging one hell of a hole here for yourself. Once she knows that, she's going to be upset."

"Why? I was keeping her safe." It truly made no sense what Jessica was saying.

"Because no woman wants to be seen as the helpless little damsel, Simon. And it's not like she's human. I mean, she's—"

"A fairy. Fighting isn't something she should have to do."

"I can make my own decisions, though, Simon." Niamh's voice echoed from the doorway.

He rose as she entered the room, her face pale though her eyes glittered with anger. "Why? Why would you take my right to make my own choices away from me? I'm here to learn and grow, not to lean on you."

Jessica winced and rose as well.

"No, stay. Please. I heard what you told him, but if there's an audience, maybe what I have to say will sink in." Niamh whirled to face him fully, having turned to address Jessica. "I'm an adult. In charge of my own life. My mistake was in thinking you had my best interests at heart when what you really were doing was setting me up so you could control me." Her chest rose and fell rapidly. "If you can't trust me to make my own decisions for myself, then I want nothing to do with you. Make a choice, Simon. Trust me and back off, or I walk out of here, never to return."

His gut clenched at the thought that she'd walk away. He couldn't possibly allow that to happen. It would be downright unthinkable.

"You two need to talk. I've got contracts to read and the phone to answer." Jess scurried from the room.

Simon watched Niamh, wondering how he could repair the damage he'd already done.

"Niamh, I placed someone in the building after I met you. Once I took control of the building, I had to place a new super in there. It made sense to add security, but once I knew who and what you were, I bulked it up. I will not apologise for wanting you safe. I'd already been speaking with James Morrow, the investigator handling the case. He raised concerns that dovetailed with those I already had. This morning, when Bailey called me, I felt like someone had shoved a fist into my chest, squeezing until I couldn't breathe. I don't want to control you. You got the job at Dr Arnett's all by yourself because Jess knew of the situation. I was only the conduit."

She nodded. "But you moved me without consultation."

"Actually, Bailey suggested it after Ulrich told him what he'd found." His gut clenched.

"And that was?"

"Bodies. A row of them hidden under a false ceiling. He smelled them and followed the trail. They were wrapped in bags. Bodies in parts, Niamh."

Now she paled. "You think...?"

He nodded. "Yeah."

*N*iamh moved to the porch when his people arrived, wanting to stay out of the way. She knew Jessica was attending the meeting, so she looked at her cell, tethered it to the computer, and opened her messaging service.

Technically, she wasn't supposed to have contact with her siblings, but Finn was the nearest in age to her, and she needed the comfort of knowing all was fine at home.

<Finn, are you there?>

<Niamh? You're not supposed to contact us. If Mam finds out, she'll be furious.>

Her fingers hovered over the keys.

<I just wanted to check everyone is fine. I miss you all.>

<We miss you too. Mam won't talk about you, but I know there's questions about why you had to leave. Danny got himself in a right twist, and Mam had to pull rank on him. He got rat-faced. Fell over in front of the elders of the herd.>

Niamh could almost see their slightly younger brother doing that. He was always the wildest of the lot. But he also had a heart of gold. She grinned at the screen, aware Finn would likely do the same. That knowledge comforted her more than she could express.

<Okay, I'll leave you, then. Just wanted to let you know I love you and miss you.>

<Is everything all right, Niamh?>

<Oh, sure. Fine. I'm starting a new job soon, and I've moved, and I've also met someone. I'll send more details soon, but I must go. Love to you and Danny and the others. Be careful and safe.>

Closing the chat window before he could respond or ask any questions, she sighed, then heard voices getting closer. Louder. Niamh scrubbed at her suddenly damp face. She and Finn had been inseparable when younger. After she was sent to America, he'd reached out to make sure she was okay. They both took great care to not get caught; otherwise, he'd face retribution from the elders. Not that she'd actually done anything wrong.

She'd found the foretelling runes and touched one by accident. The witch who'd protected their glade had told her mother a tale of the great importance of the future, and the next thing Niamh knew, she was on a plane heading far from her family.

To this day, she had no idea what her fortune had been.

Jessica stepped out. "Everything okay? It's been pretty quiet."

"Yes. I was just checking something online."

"Hmm," Jessica said and took up position beside Niamh on the end of the porch, feet dangling. "Simon's a good person, Niamh."

She waited, wondering if he'd sent Jessica out here to prepare her for something else. Something not so great. *Like maybe he's going to lock you up in a tower until he gets rid of whatever threat he thinks exists out there.*

She laughed at the whimsy, and Jessica glanced at her, a question in her eyes.

"Sorry, just a thought."

"Look, it's really none of my business, but—"

"No, it isn't, Jessica." They both jumped, as neither had heard him approach. Simon's face was stern. "You should head on home. Niamh and I should cook some dinner and have a talk."

Jessica's face tightened, and she rose. "Sure. Sorry to intrude." She was gone in a flash, her steps silent.

He advanced, and Niamh watched his every move. Not that she expected him to swoop in and hurt her but because he was a man. A very seductive one at that.

A fire lit in her belly. Hunger. Sexual hunger, she knew, because the longer she spent with Simon, the stronger she felt the need.

With great deliberation, she placed her computer onto the porch beside her and rose. She wasn't a coward, but she'd been acting like one. Treating the innocence as an excuse not to engage in what her body demanded. Telling Finn was merely the first step in acting on that need.

Her gaze rose to his. He blinked at whatever he could see on her face.

"Niamh, I know you're not ready—"

This time she took advantage, rose onto tiptoes, and kissed him, her mouth open over his.

He stilled.

With great care, she touched the tip of her tongue to his lips, felt them soften and then open, his arms winding around her midsection. She nestled in, feeling the way his body moulded to hers as if they were made for each other.

He tugged back, his breathing harsh. "Niamh—"

"Shh," she whispered. "Just enjoy."

This time he swooped in, dropping his hands to her hips as he tugged her even more firmly against him.

The hot shaft nudging at her belly showed her the level of his hunger. Her nipples were studs of physical need too, and she knew on an instinctive level that only his touch would soothe the demands of her body.

"Take me inside," she whispered.

"I... You're not ready," he answered.

On a groan, she pulled away. "I don't need you to decide for me. I'm capable of—"

He swiped a hand over his face. "Niamh, every signal you've given me until now screams needing time. That's what I'm trying to do."

The fire in her belly died down a little at his words. It was true. Until now, she'd been shying away from those intimacies. Not because she didn't want him but because she wasn't sure. Now she'd decided, and he'd backed off to give her time.

Damn it all.

She glared at him. "But, Simon, I've decided..."

He shoved his hands into his pockets and adjusted his stance. "I'm willing to give you time, but once we start, I won't stop. So take this time now. Be sure, because I want forever with you."

His words stopped her in her tracks. *Forever?*

"Hang on. I'm a fairy. You're a were... a lycan."

He nodded, eyes blazing.

"So how do we…?"

"That's something I plan on asking the fairies of the glade this weekend. And if they don't have answers, well, I'll find someone. But you're mine, Niamh, just as I'm yours. So, whatever it takes."

She blinked and nodded. Her gaze settled on the laptop, and she bent down and scooped it up. "Your meeting?"

"I'll tell you over dinner," he offered and took her hand, leading her inside.

*S*imon *growled as the cell rang, waking him from a deep sleep. He groped around, hands sliding along his nightstand. "Where the…?"*

He brought it up just in time to see the name flash, then disappear. "Damn it." Ulrich had dialled him.

Fumbling in the dark, he was about to call back when he heard creaking boards inside the house.

Muscles tensed, he rose, throwing the covers to the side. He crept to the door, using careful placement of feet from years of knowledge of the house, and peered into the hall.

A flash of white caught his attention. He thrust the door open, then stilled as Niamh turned, her face a picture of startlement. "Oh, I'm sorry. I didn't mean to wake you."

The gown she wore was sweet. White cotton with a thin band of lace edging it. Her wings fluttered.

His body firmed because beneath the flimsy gown, she wore nothing. Her shape was outlined in the dim light, nipples pink and jutting forwards against the thin material. If he looked down, he knew that wasn't all he'd see.

It took every ounce of willpower to tug his gaze back to above her collarbone. "Niamh." He reached out. "Don't be sorry."

"I didn't mean to wake you," she whispered, eyes large.

"You didn't. But you wanted something?"

She blushed. "The bathroom."

"Ahh..." Her hand fluttered to her belly and his gaze dropped, catching sight of those delicious nubs once more. He cleared his throat. "You better go to bed."

Her breath caught. "Are you asking me?" Her tone was breathless, and he glanced to her plump lips once again. He knew how they felt, the way they settled on his lips. The taste of her mouth.

He gulped, felt the movement of his Adam's apple as it bobbed.

"I would if I thought..."

A hand touched his bare chest, her pale skin a stark contrast against the sparse thatch of hairs. "Ask me, Simon."

His gut clenched, and his cock bobbed up and to attention. "When you're ready," he growled.

"I'm ready now, Simon, as I want to be with you. I've a need to feel the heat of your touch."

Unable to fight the attraction any longer, he slid his hand up to meet hers where it nestled beside his pectoral muscle. "Are you sure?"

Their gazes collided and clung. "Yes," she answered, and he moved in.

The trill of the alarm woke him, and he sat up, cursing loudly at the way his body played tricks on him. "What the fuck?"

His body was hard and tight. Needy. If she'd been beside him, he would've reached out, torn the tiny white gown from her body, and plunged into her balls deep.

Innocent! His brain screamed the reminder, and he sighed, aware that to do so like a rutting animal was not the way to proceed. Niamh deserved care and attention. Wooing. Any less wasn't acceptable. It didn't mean he wouldn't suffer for his nobility, though.

He climbed from the bed and stretched, clearing his mind of the dream and focusing on his tasks for the day.

Jessica would meet with the parents of the boys who'd annoyed the cows to finalise their community service.

Morrow was busy with his investigation, and Simon had already introduced Genevieve to him.

The plans for the formalisation of an agreement between the vamps and his pack to work with David were in the hands of his lawyers. As were plans to purchase three more properties. This time, though, he wasn't undertaking the inspection himself—they had people available to do that, as Jessica pointed out.

She'd also shortlisted the potential tenants, and he was due to scan the lists and see if he could weed out a few more.

Perhaps Niamh might be drafted to assist? An excellent idea. Spending time with her, talking.

It occurred to him that she might find his financial status overwhelming, and he needed her to understand that it wasn't a personal wealth so much as setting up the future for the pack.

He hurried into his personal bathroom, showered, and shaved. Once back in the bedroom, he dressed, choosing jeans and a comfortable shirt. Simon had no meetings, and he needed her to consider him as just another person.

He ran a hand through his hair and left the room, feeling self-conscious but hopeful.

At the bottom of the stairs, he followed sounds of movement from the kitchen and found her barefoot and in shorts and a tiny tank in the kitchen, her wings dancing as she cooked eggs and bacon in a pan. The scent of coffee filled the air, and his stomach rumbled to life.

She turned, a smile on her face. "I hope you don't mind, but I got down here and looked in the fridge, and there were many nice-looking goodies. I thought you'd appreciate a filling breakfast. The mushrooms are almost done." She swirled the small pan one last time, then took the pot off the stovetop. Two plates sat near the stove, and she spooned the large mushroom slices on the plate.

The sizzling bacon followed, as did the eggs. On the cutting board sat a loaf of fresh bread, thick slices already cut and toasted, butter melting in the warmth. "I wasn't sure if you're a tomato kind of guy, so I didn't cook any today. But if you are, next time I'll grill a few. Now, if you could pour the coffee? I brewed it just as I got started. Then we can eat."

His stomach growled again. "How did you know when to cook?"

She smiled. "I heard the shower, Simon."

He laughed, feeling comfortable with the domesticity of their situation.

Once the coffees were made, he slid them to the table, and she carried over the plates as he scooped up knives, forks, and the toast.

It was the kind of hearty breakfast he remembered his grandmother cooking for Gramps before she died.

"Is everything okay? I haven't overstepped—"

"No." He covered her hand with his. "I just remember my grandfather used to love a cooked breakfast. Grandma would do this most mornings until she died."

Her smile dimmed. "I'm sorry. That must hurt a lot. The remembering."

He shook his head. "I miss her, but no, it's a welcome memory. His new wife, Marta, isn't very good in the kitchen, so I don't suppose he's had anything like this in a long time. Perhaps the next time they visit with the kids."

Her eyes widened. "Kids?"

He laughed. "He and Marta have saddled me with a set of young aunts and uncles, and there's another on the way."

"But he's your grandfather!" She sounded shocked, and he chuckled.

"We live a long time, Niamh. Have big families over a lot of years."

"Oh..." She blinked. "That would be fun. Finn and Danny are my brothers who I'm closest to, and we used to fish and dance, gather the fruits of the forest. We'd laugh all day long. Sarah and Mary are a lot younger, and they don't understand how the three of us used to be so close. I worry about them, but at least they have Mam and Da."

"You don't talk about them much. Maybe later today you can tell me about them." He watched as her eyes sheened with tears.

"I'd really like that. If you've time."

He smiled. "We'll make time."

CHAPTER 14

He seethed. "Stupid. Stupid." He'd nearly been caught, and as it was, he'd lost everything. He'd found a new eyrie on a local building. It would not be a permanent choice, but he had to find her. The woman he'd been watching.

But she'd gone. They'd somehow moved her out of the apartment while he was busy running for his life.

There wasn't any clue where she'd gone either, except she knew the big man. The one in charge. Had he somehow spirited her away? It was possible.

"I'll have to watch."

He settled in as night fell, eyes on the apartment, watching the men and women who scurried around. The building wasn't quite full yet, though more moved in during the day.

He'd been aware that they'd been completing renovations and that as a result, every apartment was being let.

He trawled through the local social media sites and noted that the applications for tenants had closed well over a week ago. So that direction wasn't possible.

He watched the men who secured the building too. They worked in shifts, teaming up from time to time with no discernible rhyme or reason, so picking them off one by one likely wasn't an option either.

The bottle in his pocket sloshed, and he took a sip of red liquid. It only just eased the thirst that continued to build within him.

"Soon. Soon I'll find you. Then I'll feast as you suffer," he muttered.

All he had to do was find her first.

CHAPTER 15

$\mathcal{N}$iamh hurried up the steps to Dr Arnett's office as Simon waited for her to enter the building, the car's engine ticking over behind her.

The door opened, and she turned to the woman holding onto the knob. "Hi, I'm Niamh."

The woman who met her grinned. "Fabulous. I'm Lisa. You'd best come in."

Niamh turned and waved to Simon, letting him know all was well before she followed Lisa into the building.

"So, you're hanging out with the big boss man, huh?" Lisa ushered her towards the back of the room, her red ponytail swinging. "It's been the talk of the pack since we heard."

Niamh opened her mouth before shutting it again. "I, uh... Tell me about the internship," she whispered. She refused to discuss their personal relationship, not out of shame, but because that wouldn't be right.

Lisa turned away with a grin. "I think I'm going to like you," she said.

Niamh wasn't sure how to take that, but she settled into the seat Lisa indicated she take.

"Let me take you through our daily task list first. Then we can talk about the specifics of today's routine."

It was energizing to finally work in her chosen field. She had a rudimentary knowledge of medicine and healing, having taken an interest in the general health subject in her last year of formal schooling. This would be more than that. If she had any hopes of one day proving her worth as a healer, she had much to learn and experience.

Lisa was patient and happy to expand on what Niamh knew, and by the end of the day, while her head ached with knowledge, Niamh was also pleased to have achieved as much as she had.

"The first step in my new life," she told herself as she watched Lisa shutting down the systems and ensuring the security of the medication cupboards.

"We'll see you back here at eight tomorrow morning," Lisa called, and Niamh nodded, making her way down the steps where the car waited.

Even as she climbed in, she wondered what could top this.

Simon scowled as he read the report Genevieve had copied for him. The Liaison Division had taken over the investigation, given the property where the event happened was owned by the pack.

There was no definitive information as to the identity of the assailant. The only thing they knew for certain was whoever it was, they were sick. Seriously sick. The bodies—or remains in parts, as it appeared they'd found—had once been living, breathing humans. All of whom, as it now seemed, had been employed by or had kept an association with a paranormal. The missing human servant of an unhoused vampire had been among the bodies. The missing businesswoman, Julia Cummings, however, hadn't been there, and he was a little surprised by that.

"You're sure there's no hint who this may be?"

Genevieve shook her head. "None. All we know for a fact is that the perp is abducting them, torturing them, then dismembering after death. The coroner has been working overtime to identify all the bodies we've collected. But there's like fifteen at this point and room for more. We clearly interrupted him—"

"Or her?"

Genevieve shrugged. "It makes sense that it's likely a male, but we can't be 100 percent sure that's the case."

He grunted. "You also believe he's not done?"

She shook her head, and her long bob of hair swirled. "Not likely. He's—and I'll use that identifier simply for ease—escalated. We can see it in the damage on the body and the way he's dealt with the remains. The initial ones were roughly dealt with, but there's a level of refinement on the latest. The first showed bits of material, unlike on the last, which was naked. These bodies also span a longer time period, but the last few, according to the coroner, are relatively new, and the time period between the deaths is shorter in the later remains."

"Have they all been identified?"

She shook her head. "No. Because of the level of decomposition, it will take longer. They're currently checking dental records, and if necessary, we'll attempt genetic profiling."

"Fine. And have there been any more sightings?" Not that he expected there would be. If the person behind this had abandoned their lair, then maybe the interest in Niamh had passed?

"No. I doubt they'll return to the scene. There's nothing left for them there. But I have to say, the thing that really bothers me is they clearly only used the site to dispose of the corpses. This isn't their primary working area. There's no blood. No tools. Nothing hinting at what was done to them. Who knows where our perpetrators might be?"

That startled Simon. He looked up as the sound of a thudding door echoed. "We'll need to find their home base, you mean?"

Genevieve nodded, and Simon scrubbed his hand over his face, feeling weary and somehow old.

The door to his office opened, and Niamh popped in. Her hand covered her mouth. "I'm so sorry. I shouldn't have just barged in, and I'll leave you to it."

Before she could disappear, he was up and around the desk, though not before he noticed Genevieve shut the file and slide it surreptitiously into her briefcase.

"No. We're just finishing up. Genevieve, I'd like you to meet Niamh."

Genevieve stood and took her hand. "It's a pleasure to meet you. Perhaps later on we might meet and chat. I'm an officer with the Liaison Division, and I hear you were surprised at the apartments the other morning?"

Niamh's eyes grew large. "Is there something I can assist with?"

Simon tugged her close as the memory of the phone call telling him Niamh had caught sight of the murderer whistled through him, catching his nerves with jagged edges. For a moment, he inhaled just to hold the scent of her close.

"No, but later perhaps. I should go. The boss wants me there to assist with a tricky situation of breaking the news." She rose, and Simon got the distinct impression that she knew this was the first of many times Genevieve or any other shifters would be seeing the two of them together. "I'll see Jessica on my way out."

The door shut behind her, and Simon led Niamh back around the desk with him, settled into the seat, and then tugged her down so she sat on his lap.

"Simon!" Her voice rose, as if she were scandalised.

"Tell me about your day," he whispered, but not before he managed a quick swipe of his lips over hers.

She sighed and nestled in as if she'd done this many times before. "It was great, but I've got so much to learn. Lisa knows all the patients, and she walked me through the basics of the computer system. I'm not sure I'm going to be half as useful as her in under four weeks, though."

"I'm sure you'll be fine, my love. After all, she's been with Arnett for nearly twenty years."

Niamh shot bolt upright. "Twenty years? She doesn't look much over eighteen!"

He dragged her close again, resting her head on his shoulder. "She's actually fifty-four. Remember, we weres live a long, long time."

"So do fairies, you know. My mother was over two hundred when I was born."

He laughed but restrained the thought that came to mind. He didn't care if she was fifty or five hundred, so long as she stayed with him. Children would be a bonus, but at that he pulled up short, wondering if there'd ever before been a cross-species birth like theirs. He'd have to make some enquiries. Maybe if he started with Cressida? The mistress vampire was long-lived and—

The thought was short-circuited as Niamh's hands started plucking on the buttons of his shirt, then slid her hand below the material to tangle in the sparse hairs on his chest. He'd never really paid them much attention. Cara had insisted he wax them, but that hadn't been something he'd wanted to do, so he'd ignored it. Now with Niamh, she seemed to love him just as he was.

Love. The big L-word loomed over him. Was that what this was? It startled him to no end, and his back went ramrod straight.

"Simon?"

"What? Oh, I'm just trying to give you better access." He attempted a laugh that sounded false to his ears, but she read no off chord that he could tell. He exhaled, unready to investigate that emotion any further right now.

"Oh, we should stop, shouldn't we?" And indeed, her hand stopped the careful caresses she'd been giving him. The ones that warmed him all the way through to his bones, turning his guts to mush and his brain to a soggy noodle.

"Keep going." He sighed and wondered how she could have wormed herself into his emotions so quickly. Not that it mattered, because the touch of her fingers was setting fires alight in his veins.

This time when she stopped, it was to tackle another button, and he felt the cotton loosening. Then her lips found his flesh, and he exhaled while his body responded with that inconvenient and hard to ignore tenting of pants.

Gods! She'll kill me yet.

"I want to. That's where my problem lies, Simon." She slid her mouth against his flesh, and in that second, hunger roared within him.

"But I'm not sure you're ready." He cradled her head in his hand and leaned his own back into the plush leather of his seat, closing his eyes.

She pushed away, and he opened his eyes. "I am."

Two words that could change his life.

I have to be sure, make sure it's right for both of us, because this time it will mean so much more than before. I want her to enjoy it and make this a memory we'll both cherish.

Gushy much? he thought. But every bit was true.

He stopped her. "We should go out to dinner."

She wrinkled her nose, and her wings fluttered just a little. "It's hard to stay under the radar with these on your back, you know?"

He blinked and laughed. "I... Yeah, I guess. Though there are a couple places that cater for weres, and I doubt they'd be surprised."

She shook her head. "Let me cook. I do a mean chicken cordon bleu from scratch. Or I could do steak..."

"I haven't had a cordon bleu since my grandmother passed. That would be a treat."

Niamh grinned. "Then let me at your kitchen." She slipped from his lap, and losing her heat was a surprise.

"Only if you let me arrange the wine and table. Plus the dessert. I'll bet you have a sweet tooth, right?"

Her eyes drifted to half mast. "Oh God, yes."

His mouth dried at the sight of her, head back, eyes lazy, and lips spread in a soft, wide smile as if she were remembering a very pleasurable experience.

He groaned. "If you do that, we won't get to dinner."

She snapped back to awareness. "Oh... I didn't mean..." She blushed a most delightful pink.

Loping forwards, Simon slid his hands over her shoulders. "Don't apologise for remembering pleasure, Niamh." He leaned in, kissing her gently. That was only achieved by ruthlessly chaining his hunger. Tugging back, he couldn't help but be aware that his body was as hard as a boulder, and the ache felt like someone had hit him with one. *Maybe I need a cold shower.* Not the first since he'd met Niamh either.

Niamh practically skipped from the office, and he slumped down into his office seat.

Jessica breezed in with a broad grin on her face. "You look like you've been hit by Hurricane Niamh." She chuckled at her joke and sank into the chair opposite his. "Is this what mating looks like?"

He snarled. "Your turn will come."

"If it's like this, I'm running away!" Jessica's grin faded as she slid a file onto his desk. "Objections to your proposal to make me your official second."

"I'll look at them in the morning, unless there's something time sensitive?"

Jessica shook her head. "No. And by the way, I'm heading out. I have a date."

He quirked a brow. "With?"

"A big burly... vampire."

This is all just getting too confusing. "A vamp?"

She nodded. "Yep. He's got intel I want and other interesting attributes. Ones I think are worth checking out." Her eyes gleamed.

"Ahh. Then go."

"Tomorrow, then," Jessica called over her shoulder as she left.

Simon considered the file. He could open it now, but Jessica had assured him he didn't need to action anything from it immediately. He glanced to the door, more than a little aware that Niamh was busying herself in his kitchen.

Reaching down into the desk drawer, he pulled out a small black folio and flipped through the cards to find a cream pasteboard rectangle. "Emmeline's Treats and Sweets" was emblazoned on the front, covered in curlicues of gold and a phone number. He dialled and waited for the connection.

"Emmeline's Sweets and Treats. You order, we deliver. Amalia speaking."

"Hi, Amalia, this is Simon Bellingham. I'd like to place a rush order, thanks."

"Oh, hi, Mr Bellingham. Long time, no hear. Do you know what you want?"

"Yeah, I want a dessert tasting platter, delivered on the board with the matching wines. I also want a posy of flowers. Something Irish. What could you suggest?"

The woman hemmed and hawed for a moment. "Oh, I know! How about a mixed yellow? Buttercups, marigolds, and primroses. I think I have some of those on hand. Maybe even a couple chrysanthemums. Nice and cheerful. I think we still even have a green harp vase if you like."

He nodded. "Sounds perfect. How soon can you deliver? I'm still in the same location."

She must have flipped through the notes he knew were kept on the desk, as she rattled off his address after a moment.

"That's right."

"Give us an hour. I'll have it delivered to the door. How would you like to make the payment?"

It took only a few minutes to complete the order. Satisfied, he left his office, heading for the dining room.

When Frederick re-mated, he'd given Simon many of his grandmother's things, realising Marta might find another woman's memories disconcerting, though she'd insisted he didn't need to. There were tablecloths, crockery, cutlery, and even candelabra. He'd not used any since they'd come to him, but his cleaner kept on top of it all, polishing them regularly, so finding everything out didn't take long.

Once he had the table laid, with white napery and silver accoutrement, cream beeswax tapers, he nodded. "I'm going to take a shower," he called to Niamh in the kitchen, more than a little aware that everything he did right now was very homely and settled. As if they'd already moved beyond the awkward stages.

He hurried through his ablutions, wanting to see her face when she received the delivery, but took a moment to shave, brush his teeth, and don black suit pants and a crisp white shirt before heading to the kitchen.

It smelled delicious. She looked edible, and to be honest, he wasn't sure how they'd make it through the night without him spiriting her away.

"Oh, you've changed. I should too, then." She brushed down her brown pants and the cream blouse that made way for her wings. He wondered if anyone had commented during the day but dismissed it. She'd been among the paranormal anyway, Dr Arnett being a were and Lisa an elf.

The doorbell rang, and he smiled. "You should get that."

"But..." Her eyes widened. "My wings!"

Now he laughed. "Believe it or not, this entire neighbourhood is populated with a range of paras. Just the same as at Dr Arnett's. No one will think it unusual. Besides, it's a delivery I ordered. I know the family well."

"But..." she repeated.

"Go," he urged and followed her to the door, watching as she opened it, then the way her face shone when handed the vase.

"Mr Bellingham, if you could sign for the delivery?" Amalia's brother, Frank, held out the clipboard, the box with the dessert resting on top of a delivery cooler.

He did and took control of the box, then ushered Niamh back inside. "Like them?"

She turned, face shining and eyes wet.

He gulped. "I didn't mean to make you cry. I'm sorry." *Stuffed it up, you fool.*

Niamh sniffled. "I'm crying because this means so much. Thank you." She lifted onto her tiptoes and kissed him. He nearly dropped the box, but it restored his faith in his own planning skills.

He followed her to the kitchen, and she set the vase on the side. "We should take that out to the dining room after," Niamh offered.

She set to work, plating their food, and he unwrapped the box, aware that they used cooling packs to keep the temperatures down, but he still wanted to get the platter into the fridge before their effectiveness wore off.

When Niamh glanced over, she gasped. "How much chocolate is there?"

Simon laughed. "Not as much as you'd think. A lot of this is made with fruits to get the depth of colour. But if you have a problem with chocolate..." He popped a chocolate-covered grape into his mouth and moaned.

"Stop that!" Niamh laughed and whacked him with the tea towel. As she returned the pan to the oven, she opened the fridge door for him, and he slid the tray of confections inside. "Now let's take these through to the dining room."

"Wait!"

She turned. "What?"

"The wine." He'd stashed several bottles in the fridge. He found a French champagne, then reached into the freezer to fill an ice bucket he'd pulled out of a cupboard along with two matching flutes. "Now we're ready."

*I*t didn't matter about the dinner. Or the wine. The dessert could have been sawdust for all Niamh cared, because tonight, she knew they'd commit themselves one to the other. It lay in the air. A visceral knowing. Carnal and hungry.

She ate, and they talked of the mundanity of life.

It was all a smokescreen. The prelude to the *pas de deux*.

When the meal was done, she sat there, the bubbles popping on her tongue from the champagne, and waiting for his move.

"Come." He spoke with a commanding tone, and she rose, following Simon up the steps to the room she'd not yet entered.

At the door, he stopped and filled it, barred it personally with his body. "Be sure, Niamh, because I don't think I could change my mind once we begin."

"I don't want you to, Simon. I know of the actions of lovemaking, but it's with you I wish to share it." Her wings fluttered wildly, betraying the pulse of her heartbeat.

This time when he moved, he flowed over her. Around her. Surrounding and demanding.

Her body ached for the connection.

He ran a hand down her side, and she leaned in, wanting more.

His other arm surrounded her waist, travelled up to the spot where the sinews and bone of her wing met the flesh of her back. He stroked with long purposeful touches. and she felt the heat rising in her body, melting the hunger between her legs.

"Simon." She sighed.

She reached for his shirt, popping the first and then second button while he growled.

With extreme care, he slid his hand beneath the fine material of her shirt, and she keened as her body clenched and tensed with hunger.

"I'm afraid to hurt you, Niamh. Take off that shirt."

Their gazes met, and she knew what it cost him to make that comment. With unsteady fingers, she released the fasteners and slid the blouse to the floor. He hissed in reaction, a tide of scarlet flushing his skin.

"Gods," he muttered and cupped her cheek. Niamh nuzzled in. "I've wanted this since I met you."

"And now the time is here." She reached behind herself, aware that it pushed her breasts up and out. Knew he watched, and that pleased her further, that he wanted what she offered freely.

The clips of her bra slid free, and she let the scrap of material fall to the floor unheeded.

His hand shook as he touched her skin. She hissed as the frisson of awareness ricocheted from chest to groin and back out to every extremity. She reached out for his shirt, but he backed away, holding her eyes captive as he released the buttons.

As inch by delicious inch was uncovered, she had to clench her legs together as the desire took over. Her nipples peaked, and she knew he noticed when he dropped his gaze to them.

"Touch me. I'm yours," Niamh whispered.

He reached out, sliding a finger down over the slight curve of her breast, found the areola, and circled it.

Her legs locked, eyes blinded as pleasure took wing.

His mouth followed the path of his touch, lips nipping and tongue flicking the bud he discovered, and she cried out with the pleasure that spiralled mindlessly around her brain.

Once his mouth moved, the only sound apart from their breathing was the beating of her wings.

Gasping for air and tugging away, because she'd surely explode before they even reached the irrevocable step, Niamh reached for her pants, sliding them and her panties down her legs so that finally she was bare before him.

Simon's Adam's apple bobbed.

"Gods..." He groaned and shucked his own clothes in a quick, urgent move. "How do I love you without hurting you?"

"Come," she urged. "Come to me."

He did, his cock an urgent and hard pulsing jut of sinew and skin. Angry red with carnal need.

Placing her hands on his shoulders, feeling the tension and power of him, should have left her running, but it didn't. He'd never hurt her. Instead, she wrapped a leg around his waist. "This time we love like this," she explained, the knowing instinctive.

With a grunt, he hoisted her up and her other leg joined the first around his waist, tugging him close so he nudged against her entrance.

One thrust was all it would take, she knew.

Niamh prepared herself for the pain, knew that was necessary to achieve the pleasure, and impaled herself. Her vision turned red for a moment. She arched and waited, hoping the pain would pass soon.

She knew he worked to control his reactions, fingers digging deeply into the flesh of her waist, holding her hips. "Niamh, I can't hold on much longer."

"A. Minute. More," she whimpered, and then the urgency surged. With a small nudge, she moved, and he groaned.

"Mine," Simon growled.

"Yes," she cooed. Now that the pain had receded, the pleasure bloomed once more. She rocked her hips against him and felt the magic winding around them both while her wings beat furiously in the tempo of their thrusts.

Eyes closed, she basked in the glory of their joining.

"Simon," she called, feeling the coiling spring within her, demanding and driving her undulations to become wilder and more demanding.

His fingers bit into her soft flesh, and she wanted—no, *needed* more.

Their dance was wild. Furious even as they moved together, flowing in and out, up and down.

"Simon!" she cried as the pleasure crashed down around her, and her head bumped against something hard.

Unable to help herself, she opened her eyes and realised her wings had carried them both up so they brushed against the ceiling.

Simon moved urgently now, demanding and thrusting, taking what he needed. She watched him, letting her wings hold them in place until he grunted, shook, and emptied himself within her.

Now she let them sink back down, settled them on the bed, bodies still entwined, caressed by the whisper of the night air.

"How?"

She grinned at his soft demand. Knew he meant the flight of lovers they'd just taken. Now wasn't the time to explain it all. She simply wrapped her arms around him, feeling a sense of completion she'd never before experienced.

"I'll explain later." She yawned as lethargy stole over her figure.

"Niamh?"

"Sleep now. Talk later." She truly didn't have the energy to explain now, the demands on her body having exhausted her.

She closed her eyes and let sleep claim her, but not before she thought she heard him whisper against her hair, "My mate. My love. Forever."

CHAPTER 16

*H*e didn't like being beaten, but somehow she'd escaped him. The woman he'd tried to claim twice now. She had to be more than human, he decided, given the way the weres protected her.

Just like the ones before, she was an unhoused other.

"I'll find you, my dear." He always did, no matter where she'd hidden.

For now, he hunkered down, thanking his forward planning for giving him the chance to rent this small house on the outskirts of town.

It wasn't perfect, but there was a shed out back. It was private enough for his playroom, and besides, previously he kept them gagged until the last game started, but now that changed. He would take them to the forest, to the lair he'd dug deep within the trees.

"Where no one will find me." The words were a cackle, but no one would hear. Not here. He was careful and canny.

He'd finally taken care of his last toys. They hadn't been nearly as satisfying, now that he had a new target, so he'd discarded them like the trash they'd become.

He turned in a slow, appraising circle. This place was off the beaten track. He accepted the sounds that might carry , but given his new surroundings, they caused no issues.

He'd find her again. "Then we'll play."

For now, though, he would find a substitute or two, and he'd make do.

CHAPTER 17

Waking with Niamh in his arms felt amazing. It was as if all the others Simon had been with melted away in the heat of a summer's morning.

Her wings had beaten so fast, the iridescent glow they'd emitted brighter than ever before. Her entire body had lit up with a glow from deep inside her. Was it the intensity of her emotions? The pleasure?

He didn't know. Frankly, as far as he was concerned, these things were specific to Niamh, and Simon embraced that. Embraced her.

Loved her.

That she was a fairy might cause some issues, but they'd remain together. They'd construct a way to make it happen. Together.

With a light touch, he traced his fingers over her wings, the veins of purples and pinks soft now. The membrane of the wings themselves was near translucent.

She moaned in her sleep, legs moving as he continued his exploration. Small protrusions extended from her back, joining the sinews and membrane to her body.

He slid his fingers over them and her eyes shot open, shining, as did her entire body now. "Simon," she gasped, body arching.

It fascinated him that she could be so responsive. He leaned in for a kiss, but she was there first, devouring and demanding.

She flowed over him, her small breasts grazing his chest, and he couldn't help the exhalation of pleasure. "Gods, Niamh, what you do to me."

His cock had quickly gone from somnolent to engorged, and he raised his leg, gently abrading the apex of her thighs. Finding it already dampened with desire, his hands moved instinctively to take hold.

His mouth found a budding nipple and laved it while she wound her hands in his hair.

Desire roared within him. He captured her hips, aligning them, while he tore away from the pleasure of her body, blindly finding her mouth.

He plunged so deep that knowing where his body ended and hers began was impossible. The rhythm of the beating of her wings, the cadence of his movements, each designed to bring them maximum fulfillment.

"Please, Simon, love me," she demanded, ripping her mouth from his and swallowing a lungful of oxygen as he did the same.

"I do. I will. Mine, Niamh. Only mine." His incisors descended, and he fought hard with his creature to not pierce her neck, not take what it demanded.

Mine. Make her one of us.

I will not take her choices from her, he countered.

Instead, he gloried in the sensations of loving. Feeling her body tighten, he opened his eyes to watch the flash of light that emanated from her at the point of orgasm, her body a glove around his.

"Simon..." The breathy exhalation brushed his skin as he found completion and roared with pleasure.

They fluttered down gently and once more found themselves entwined on the bed.

"That's amazing, Niamh."

She blushed a little. It entranced him to find the rosy glow extended down to her breasts. He touched the warming flesh with a careful fingertip.

"I've never done that before with anyone. Loving... It should mean something," she murmured.

"Yes," he agreed, cupping her face and bringing her closer. "It should. This time it does."

Niamh frowned. "Last time it didn't?"

His brow wrinkled, wondering how to explain that beforehand, he'd allowed himself to seek pleasure without the extension of the authentic emotion. "Not with you, Niamh. With you, it's deep. I don't want to let you go. I crave you. With the others, there was pleasure, but unlike this. It's hard to explain."

She nodded. "Okay. I understand now. I mean..." She scrunched up her face. "Many fairies use lovemaking as a pleasurable pastime. I've heard they use the flash of this pleasure like a drug, but the indiscriminate sexual activity blinds us to what can be. According to my grandmother, to wait for that connection, it allows us to see clearly, to feel more fully, and achieve a true enlightenment that very few experience."

"That flash of light?"

She grinned. "I... Grandmother told me of it. 'When true emotion glows, we have chosen well.'" With a cough, she moved away. "My grandmother taught me the old lore. The rules we should live by so we may be happy in ourselves, lend the earth the help it needs. That kind of thing."

He slid a curl of hair from her face. "If the lore says that, then who are we to argue?"

She gulped. "But I've never heard of a were and a fairy. I mean..."

"Shhh," he whispered, though he also worried about that. It seemed incongruous that they might be a pair, yet so very different. She was fragile and soft, him hard, driven, and tasked with the responsibility of looking after the entire pack.

His alarm trilled, and he grunted, wishing they could stay there together, but it was Niamh's second day in Dr Arnett's office, and he had much to do. He added an extra task: talk to Cressida. It moved to the top of the list.

They rose, and he watched as she flitted about, unconcerned by her nudity. He now saw a more playful and unrestrained side.

"I need clothes." Opening the door to the hall, she strode away, and he gulped, catching sight of her curved derriere and the flitter of wings as she rose. Today they shone with purples and yellows and blues, as if they radiated her emotions.

The L-word loomed again, and this time he embraced it. Soon. He'd tell her soon. They'd go somewhere special, perhaps back to the glade? They'd make a day of it. Once he knew how to go forwards.

He showered quickly and then started with surprise when he returned to find her sitting on his bed, the covers returned to an orderly fashion.

She bit her lip. "I need advice."

His brow quirked. "What about?"

"Fairy things," she muttered, tracing a finger over the bold design of the coverlet.

"About us?"

She shrugged. "Yes and no." When Niamh looked up, he read concern on her brow, creases there that hadn't been earlier.

"What about your mother?"

"Mam? I'm not allowed contact. The banishment was very specific. No calls to Mam or Da. No texts or messages of any kind, not even from my family. Not until what will be passes."

A single tear clung to the tips of her eyelashes.

He dropped the towel and lowered to his knees before her. It cut him to ribbons seeing the pain on her face. "I don't know why they'd send you away, Niamh, and I can't understand the pain you're experiencing, but I will give you everything I can. I will be there for you."

She gave a soggy sniff. "I know. I'm not daft enough to think this is forever, but when I need her the most, we can't even communicate, and I don't know why." She swiped at the tear, but another took its place. "It hurts me."

Simon gathered her close, letting her scent and the feel of her soothe his own ragged emotions. Seeing the pain she wore? He felt it just as keenly and needed to comfort her. To take just a small amount would give him no greater fulfillment.

When Niamh pulled away, he let her go, aware that not only was time limited but also that she intended to stand on her own. Not that she had to—all that was necessary was to ask—but she'd accepted the terms of this banishment. Gods, how that irked him!

"I need to get ready for work," she muttered and shook her head. Her wings had dimmed, and now they were a dull colour.

"Do your wings change colour a lot?"

She glanced at him through her eyelashes. "Why?"

He smoothed a hand over Niamh's cheek. "Earlier they were radiant. Now they're not so much."

She sighed. "Yes, they show our emotional state. It's hard when you're among fairies to keep a secret, or to be happy about something around another who isn't. It's such a giveaway!"

He laughed then, and she did too. He noted the slight lightening of the colour in her wings. "Well, I guess there'll be no keeping secrets from me either."

She scowled. "I guess not, you observant creature you."

"Hungry creature," he growled with a mock intensity, and her laughter tinkled around them.

"Come downstairs and I'll feed you, and then you can take me to work... or I can walk."

He shook his head. "I'll drive you wherever you need to go."

"Is it hard?"

He stopped on the steps beside her. "What?"

"Learning to drive. Is it hard?"

He stared. "You don't know how to drive?"

She shook her head. "There was never any need in Ireland. We stuck pretty much to our forests and glades, flew where we needed to go. When I went to the airport, one of the witches drove, as I never learned."

His mind whirred. "Then I'll teach you. Get you a car so you can come and go as you want to."

Now she looked dumbfounded. "You don't need to buy me a car."

He brushed off her worries. He'd find one small enough that it wouldn't be too heavy for her to handle but still strong and sturdy.

"Don't worry about it, Niamh. Now, I'm hungry."

She rolled her eyes with exaggerated frustration. "What's new?"

Finally back at his desk, coffee in hand, Simon stared at the screen. Cressida. He'd known her for a long time. She'd recently became the overlord of the vampires, and her life partner had assumed her role as councillor. What would she have to say? He also knew the power of the overlord overcame the fire of the sun. While it was another form of magic, he knew—or had recently learned—that they all stemmed from a single source of power.

Simon sucked in a deep breath and reached for his cell.

"Hello?" a female voice answered after several rings.

"Cressida? It's Simon Bellingham. I'm wondering if you have a few moments?"

"Simon! Hi, yes. Samantha is asleep and so is Daniel, so I'm just trying to catch up on paperwork."

"Never seems to end, does it?" He laughed, as did she.

"No. But what can I help you with?"

His mirth died away. "Fairies. I need to know more. Their lore, the process of banishment, and why a witch would seek to have one removed. Mating."

"Wow. That's quite a list, Simon. Backtrack for a moment, though. Why do you suddenly need this information?"

It felt wrong to tell her he'd fallen for one. He hadn't even told Niamh yet, but he needed the information. "I've met one. She's..." He stumbled over the way to describe her. Happy usually, driven and loyal, beautiful and fragile.

His.

"You've found a mate," Cressida deduced. "She's a fairy, I take it."

He grunted.

"I can see why you're confused. In all my years, I've never heard of a fairy-were mating before. But then, who'd have heard of a vamp-were hybrid like Jelani either? I'm sorry I can't give you any further clarity. I'll look through the library I had brought here from Gianna's stronghold. There may be something there, but I'd advise that you talk with an elder of a fairy herd. They may shed more light on it. The one thing I know is that there is a change in the magic. As if the very essence has reshaped itself."

Scrubbing a hand over his brow, he considered her words. "How do you manage it? Being overlord, mother, and life partner?"

"It's all about balance and honesty, Simon. But you have to find your own, because what works for us may well be different for you."

"Yeah." He looked out the window and noted that Jessica was arriving. "I have to go, Cressida. I'll think over your suggestions and will be in touch again soon."

They disconnected, and he sat back in his seat, drumming his fingers on the tabletop as he considered all she'd said. The only logical conclusion was to talk to an elder fairy.

Niamh bounced out of work and hurried down the steps, looking for Simon. A small compact sat idling on the side, and it was only when she bent down that she realised it was Simon at the wheel.

She stopped, opened her mouth, then closed it again.

"Come on, get in."

She did as he insisted and inhaled the scent of... new car? "What are you doing?"

"Taking you for your first driving lesson," he answered. "Seat belt on first, though."

"The car?"

"Is yours. I had it registered in your name, the insurance is good for a year, and—"

"Wait," she cried. "I don't have a learner's permit even."

"We're going to do the paperwork today." He handed her a book. "Start reading."

She glared at him. "You're joking!"

He shook his head. "You need a vehicle, and now you have one. You need a license to drive it, so we're going to make it happen. I know you've got a quick memory. If you can pull this off, we can have you licensed and prepared to get on the road in no time."

She grizzled but opened the booklet at the pages he'd tagged. "These are the important pages, I take it?"

He nodded, and they drove for what felt like ages. When he stopped, he grabbed a light jacket from the back and passed it to her. "You'll need this. There's the odd non-para who uses this office, so you must be careful."

She shrugged it on, then climbed out and allowed him to lead her as she kept reading and into the office.

"I got you an appointment with a friend of mine," he said and waved a hand at an older woman who'd just exited an office to the side.

"Lord, it's good to see you again. This is the woman you spoke of?"

Niamh took a moment to inspect the woman. She was young and trim, but there was an edge to her voice.

"Yes. Niamh, I'd like you to meet Alara. She owes me a favour or four."

Alara's smile was more of a grimace. "You'd best come into my office."

They entered the room, and Simon took the book from Niamh's hands.

"But I'm not finished."

"You'll be fine," he soothed and settled down beside her.

Alara's eyes followed his movements, and the woman sighed. "Do you have identification on you?"

Niamh retrieved her passport from her purse and handed it over.

"An Irish citizen, hmm? And your address?"

Simon answered that question, and soon the paperwork was complete. It surprised Niamh when a sheet of paper slid towards her.

"You need to answer these questions without help." Alara speared Simon with a look that told him if he interfered, there'd be problems.

He raised both hands and settled back. Not that Niamh was in the least convinced he'd prefer to be the one assisting.

Niamh worked her way through the sheet of paper. None of the questions appeared overly difficult. She could see one or two that may cause issues, but she'd only just read her way through the guidebook and they were fresh in her memory. The signs were different than those in her own country, but despite that, she'd seen them often enough during her time here.

She answered the last question and slid the sheet back.

Alara picked up the marking guide and ran through them. "Well done. Then we best go do the payment and photo. Your temporary permit will be good until your permanent one turns up in the mail."

Niamh followed, shocked she'd achieved so much in a short time. The room was emptying, and that gave her some satisfaction. At the window, she paid the money, and Alara handed over the completed test to the cashier. Out of the corner of her eye, Niamh caught sight of one or two who watched, and it became clear that this wasn't the usual flow of paperwork.

She then had a photo taken, received a piece of paper with instructions on how to sit for her driver's test and the process, then another that the woman called a temp license.

Simon walked her through the double doors to the car. "Want to have your first lesson?"

She shook her head. "It's nearly dark, and my head feels like it's going to explode."

He laughed as they climbed into the car. "Okay. This one time. But from here on in, I'm going to make you drive and learn the car, the rules, and get comfortable. I want you to feel in control of your life, Niamh." He gathered her close, or as close as the gearshift would allow. "That's why I pushed today. Once you have your license, you'll be able to come and go as you choose."

"So I don't have to rely on you."

He shook his head. "No. So you can do what you want. Not that I don't want you around, because I do. But I want you to feel free enough to choose to be with me."

His words made sense, but it was as if he were already untangling the strings between them. Had she been too clingy? Done something wrong?

"No, Niamh. I'm learning to read your emotions, love. There's no underlying agenda. I want you and always will. Now let's go home. We can cook dinner, then sit outside watching the night sky, or we could watch a movie or just cuddle. Whatever you want."

She bit her lip. "I'd like a shower first, and then we can cook dinner. Then we'll decide. Together."

Her cell beeped, and she fished around in her bag and pulled it out. Her hand went to her mouth.

"What's wrong?" Simon's voice had deepened, and concern flashed over his face.

"Danny and Finn. They've been banished. They're on their way to America."

Her gut roiled. *What could they have done?*

"We've spare rooms," Simon said matter-of-factly. "We'll move your things into my room. It's where I'd like you to be anyway."

She glanced at him, her heart filling to bursting. "Really?"

He reached over and took her hand in his. "Yes, Niamh. I mean it. So when do they arrive?"

She glanced at the text. "Midnight."

"Then we'd better go home. You can change, we'll eat, and then head out to meet them at the airport. Can you text them?"

Niamh bit her lip. "I can. I mean, I'm not supposed to have contact, but we..." A thought flashed through her mind. "What if that's what happened? Mam and Da found out that we remained in contact?"

"We'll sort that once they're here. Concentrate on what we can do. Fix the rest later."

She nodded, her hands tightly bunched together.

Simon read the concern on Niamh's face. He'd do just about anything he could to ease it. During the evening, she'd quieted, and now she stood beside him, her hand clasped in his as they waited for the great enormous doors to open, releasing those on the Dublin flight.

She wore jeans and a white shirt, her wings safely obscured by a long brown leather coat matching her knee-high boots. Men glanced at her as they passed her by, but she was oblivious.

The whoosh echoed in the busy arrivals area, and she scrunched in closer. He slid his arm around her waist, feeling the tension. "They'll be here soon, Niamh."

She answered with an abstracted nod, craning over the crowds.

They thinned as people found the connections waiting for them.

Suddenly she cried out and hurried forwards, Simon shadowing as she zigzagged around people. Two young men, their features so similar to hers, drooped until they heard her call their names.

She launched at them, and their arms closed around her. Her family. Those she was closest to had reunited with her. She sobbed now, and he moved up, touching her back lightly. "Niamh, let's get them to the car."

The biggest and burliest of them straightened, his face set with agitation. "Who are you, and what are you doing with our Niamh?"

"Oh..." She tugged away and settled in his arms, and Simon sighed, understanding the concern.

"I'm Simon. You're coming home with us."

"Us?" the other brother parroted.

"Aye," Niamh answered. "Simon and I... we're..."

"Together," Simon finished, not yet willing to share that she'd be his for eternity if she would allow.

"Simon, this is Finn." She pointed to the burly one. "And Danny." The one who'd questioned their togetherness.

Simon glanced down at their single suitcase each and backpack. "Is that it?"

They nodded.

Niamh bit her lip. "I…"

"Later," Simon repeated. "Let's get to the car. I'm sure you're exhausted."

They followed as Niamh and Simon took the lead, hands once more entwined. He opened the large black SUV back and stashed the suitcases. It was a sorry sight, Simon thought, when all their belongings filled a single bag and backpack.

Niamh climbed into the front, and the two men took up position in the back.

"So, what happened?" She turned to look at them.

A stomach growled, and Simon smiled. "Who's hungry?"

The two men chorused, and Niamh grimaced. "They're always hungry."

He took them through a drive-through and ordered coffee for himself, tea for Niamh, and two meals for the men in the back. They ate and drank their way home.

By the time they'd settled the brothers into their rooms, it was nearly two in the morning, and Niamh was dragging.

"Your sister has to work this morning, so how about we hold off discussions until tonight? We'll all head to bed, and if you wake before I drop her to the office, you can catch up then?"

With heads drooping, the four climbed the stairs. It was only when Finn and Danny realised they were sharing a bedroom that their stares narrowed. "Where are you sleeping, Niamh?" Finn growled.

"With Simon," she answered quietly with a smile, then bade them goodnight.

He shut the door so they once more had their privacy. "Are you okay with this?"

"You don't want to share with me?" Niamh countered with a saucy grin.

"My bed is your bed, Niamh. You're my home now."

Her eyes widened. "I…"

"Let's go to bed."

He stripped and climbed under the covers, and she did the same. He gave a sigh of contentment when she settled in his arms, her wings tucked back.

He stroked one, and she arched. "Simon, shouldn't we sleep?"

"Yes, my Niamh. We should sleep."

CHAPTER 18

imon Bellingham. He glanced at the photo on the screen. He knew where the girl was. His prize. The toy he sought above all.

He sniffed the cape she'd lost—which he now held in his grasp. It smelled like a fresh field, buttercups, and cinnamon all in one delightful package.

The man in the picture had spirited her away. But he'd find him, and then he'd find the girl. He didn't know her name, but in his memory, he could draw up an image of her face.

Slight with a pronounced jaw, sparkling eyes, and hair an indeterminate shade of blond.

"Mine," he rasped as he strode forwards down the road.

He'd learned all he could from the woman who'd lived next door to her. He hadn't bothered with a name. She didn't need one.

Would never need one once he'd completed his game with her.

Now the driving need to prepare was upon him.

"I rather like the chase, so perhaps next time that should be part of it."

Once settled in the car, he turned for his new home and the lair he'd prepared.

CHAPTER 19

Simon worked steadily, more than a little aware that Finn and Danny were in his house, inspecting his life and testing whether he was good enough for their sister.

He couldn't blame them. If he had a sister, he'd likely be the same.

The file Jessica had slid before him sat waiting for his inspection. He opened it and began reading through the emails that had come in after the Council meeting.

Not that he had to take their advice. He was Lord of Lycans and more than capable of making these decisions, but Jessica had proven herself repeatedly.

She was worthy and strong, diligent and well respected. Not one of them could step into the position, and none of them objected on any other ground except her gender.

"Jess!" he called.

She walked into his office. "Yes?"

"I've read them. They're all rubbish. We'll address it at the next Council meeting, but none of the objections hold water."

"But, Simon, they can make your life difficult."

He rose and stalked to the bookshelf, rifled through it until he took up a book: *The Lore and Law of the Lycan* by Samuel MacPherson.

Without a word, Simon handed it over. "Read the chapter entitled 'The Lord and his Entourage.'"

Jessica blinked but dutifully flicked through until she reached the chapter halfway through the tome. "The Lord is above all, the master, and controls the decision-making of the pack. He alone takes responsibility, but also, he alone chooses those who council him. The Lord shall take advisors as he sees fit, depending entirely on their effectiveness to fill the role."

"He decides. He is responsible. You are the best fit, Jess."

Her eyes watered. "Wow. I never thought I'd be in the position. I mean until now, it's been only men."

"But times are changing, Jess. I trust you. You know the pack and have their respect. You're capable and have a good head on your shoulders."

Jessica laughed. "And an older head too, remember? I'm older than you."

Simon snorted. "Only by about seventeen years. That doesn't make you old."

She shook her head. "No. I'm not old. What if I want a family though?"

"We'll make it work. You can take some time for family commitments, but we work around it. The pack is big enough to find the support you'd need on the home front."

His cell beeped, and he cursed, but it was Morrow's number. "Simon speaking," he answered.

"I've got a lead. It's tenuous but tied to a house. Can we meet?"

"Yeah. Name the place and time. I'll be there with my second."

Jessica's eyes widened. "What?" she mouthed.

He scribbled down the directions, not answering Jessica immediately. Only once he'd disconnected did he look up. "I want you there, Jess. You're my other eyes and ears. You might know someone, or your friend the vamp may."

She grimaced. "Okay, but I'm not so sure about this."

He ushered her out the door, calling to Finn and Danny that they'd be back and to make themselves comfortable. They'd have to talk soon, but right now, the concern was to find the person who'd almost abducted Niamh and murdered the fifteen they'd found on the rooftop.

It wasn't far to the coffee shop where Morrow had said they should meet. Once they'd parked the car, they headed in, ordered coffees, and settled at a table to the rear of the shop.

"We should have brought Genevieve in on this too," Jessica said.

He'd already decided once they'd met with Morrow, tested what he had to say, that he should get her involved. It wasn't so much that he didn't trust her, because indeed he did, but that he needed to keep this whole thing quiet. Vamps dealt with things in-house, and Simon could see the efficiency in that.

If they could put together a decent case, gather enough evidence, he planned to petition the state and later on the central government to allow them the same freedoms. They weren't like humans. The situations were unique. Whether it be were-lust or murder, what drove them was the animal inside. Something no human could understand.

"You've got something going on in your head. Ready to share?"

He glanced at Jessica. "The vamps. They can cope with their own issues internally. If this is a were—not that I can say that with surety yet, just that it's what I think—we should deal with them ourselves. Set up our own judicial process. Humans don't understand the complexity of our dual natures. The animal within and the man or woman who controls them."

"That makes sense, so far."

"But we need to prove that we can not only examine the transgressions but also deal with them. To pass effective judgement. Most times, we can re-educate, which would always be the first choice. Others are beyond that. Remember the case with Ruaan Beledes?"

"Ugh." Jessica grunted. "She ate her husband."

He nodded. "The only logical action was to put her down. When she escaped, they found her with other bodies. The animal had taken over. She had no ability or desire to control the urges. She declared herself a man-eater."

"What happened with her in the end?"

He grunted. "Electric chair. I attended as Lord of Lycans. But if she'd faced her peers, it would have been sooner. Those who lost loved ones would've had the right to justice in a way that was appropriate."

Jess traced the pattern on the tablecloth. "You think we can put up an argument?"

"I think with the backing of Cressida and the other known paras, we could. So long as we're united."

The door rattled, and they both looked up to see Morrow striding through. He ordered and waited for his coffee, then settled down at the table, his glance to Jessica telling.

"My second in charge, Jessica," Simon explained.

They shook hands, though Jessica did frown at the touch.

"So, what do you know?"

Morrow sighed and tugged some papers from his suit. "I found out the warehouse that the perp was using belongs to one of the vamp nests. A little digging"—Morrow grinned—"brought a name to light. Simeon Caldwell. He's a lower-level drone with the House of Tudor."

Simon frowned. "That's Hope and Xavier's house."

"And run by her father for a long time as *Yeux Secondes*. A dangerous and destructive man. He gave this to Caldwell to handle. Caldwell signed a lease to an Albert Persible. A were and known admirer of your friend Julien Delacorte."

Simon snarled. "Bastard."

Morrow inhaled. "He's since taken off. We don't know where currently. We're digging through the other leases Caldwell handled. But we need Xavier to open the books."

"I'll talk with Cressida. She must approach Xavier. I can't ask directly, as that violates certain agreements." *Circles within circles,* Simon thought, every part of this harder because the old ways were so entrenched.

Jessica frowned. "But who else knows about Julien Delacorte and Persible? And any connection?"

Morrow smiled. "That's just it. I found someone who knows someone, and they squawked. Persible forgot to make the pay-offs, and that helps us. But one other piece of information?"

Simon cocked his head to the side. "What?"

"He's crazy. Certifiable. But also brilliant. Whoever goes after him will have to be careful." Morrow took a last sip of his coffee. "The coroner dealing with the bodies is in the hospital. The remains were coated with thallium. He's in intensive care with multiple organ failure. Thallium can be absorbed through the skin. Touching anything he's dosed could be catastrophic to humans. We don't know what it would do to a para."

"So, that really complicates things a lot. Anyone who goes out will need to wear gloves," Jessica murmured.

"And a mask. Inhalation is also an issue. This stuff is a by-product from the refining of heavy-metal sulphide ores," Morrow added.

"So, what? We need to investigate smelters?" Simon's hand clenched into a fist.

"I don't believe that's where he came across it. It's also used in glass production and pharmaceuticals. The ones the House of Tudor has an interest in would certainly be utilising this compound."

"What in heaven's name would they be using thallium for if it's toxic?"

Morrow opened his notepad. "Thallium chloride is used to show the blood flow inside the heart during exercise and rest. When injected, it's used to image the thyroid for abnormalities, and the parathyroid and the brain for signs of tumours."

Simon blinked. "Right, so probably not commonly available, then?"

Morrow shook his head. "No, you can't just buy it at the drugstore."

"All right. As soon as I get back to my office, I'll..." He chanced a look at his watch. "Tonight, I'll contact Cressida. Get her help. Meanwhile, have you got someone watching Persible?"

"Yes, I've got men monitoring his movements and someone else checking his phone records." Morrow rose. "Watch your girl. That he had not one but two attempts at her—"

"What?" That struck Simon hard. "I only know of one..."

"Before you were on the scene, she was late to work. Someone made a play for her. Stole her covering, and she had to loiter in a park until her supervisor, Ellen, came for her."

A rumble started in Simon's chest. She'd been in danger and had said nothing. A red mist settled over him. He had to brush it aside, because he hadn't told her about the investigation either.

He'd rectify that. Tonight.

*N*iamh dawdled today to the car. Work had been... okay. One patient she'd seen for the first time today had doused her with sadness.

A child of four with an incurable disease had dropped in for a check-up. Her mother remained stoic though clearly struggling while the little girl sat on her lap, book in hand, waiting with a patience most adults couldn't exhibit.

Until now, she'd been so high on the fact that she was attaining her desired life, she'd lost sight that some illnesses were incurable.

Niamh hid in the consulting room after clearing it. The sniffles were hard to hide, along with the droop of her wings.

The door opened, and Dr Arnett entered. "Are you all right, Niamh?"

She turned and choked back a sob. "No. I don't get how a child can be so ill. Dying. It's wrong."

Dr Arnett came closer. "We can't heal everyone. Medicine and healing are a science, not magic. It hurts every time I have to tell a parent their child won't survive, Niamh. I can't lie to you. They each take a chunk of your heart, and it's so damn hard. Especially when you delivered the child, cared for them through their infancy. But it's also rewarding to know you're able to ease their last days. It's the blessing we receive too."

She sat down in her consulting chair and invited Niamh to take the seat opposite.

"So, are you on any form of contraceptive?"

Niamh looked at her. "What's that?"

"Bloody fairies," Dr Arnett muttered. "It's a medication you take daily to stop yourself from conceiving a child."

Niamh blinked. "But I'm a fairy. We don't do those sorts of things."

"And normally you wouldn't be with a shifter or were. Especially not the Lord of Lycans. Has he bitten you?"

"What? No!" Niamh half rose from the chair, but Dr Arnett made her sit again with a pointed finger.

"I've not had a lot to do with fairies. You guys usually go it alone, but your biology is simple. So, since you're here, you get an exam, and then I'll prescribe you a course of contraceptives. I take it you and Simon are together?" She waved her hand, and Niamh could discern exactly what she was asking.

Niamh blushed. "Well, only just, but yes."

Now, standing beside the car and peering in, she realised Simon was frowning. "What's wrong?" he asked.

She shook her head and climbed in, the box of tablets hidden within her pocket while her bag, too small to conceal something like that, rested on the floor at her feet. Dr Arnett had been cautious, telling her there could be side effects and to inform her of any immediately, but of course, Simon didn't need to know that yet.

"Niamh?" Simon prompted.

"Something to do with work. It was sad, and Dr Arnett told me there'd be days like this." The answer was as much as she could share, as Dr Arnett had also been firm that she couldn't disclose what went on in the practice, not even with Simon.

"Finn and Danny are practically climbing the wall. By the way, when were you going to tell me that someone had attempted to abduct you beforehand?" Simon had kept his words calm, but she jumped.

"Oh... I forgot. I mean, I was really stressed about my job situation, then the move and you and me... It slipped my mind. Besides, it was before we'd met."

"If I'd known, I would have put a tracker on you," he growled.

Her hackles went up. "I'm not a toy you can lose. I'm a woman."

"Yes," he replied. "And a madman has targeted you twice now. Not just that, he's poisoned the coroner dealing with the case by coating the body parts with thallium."

"I don't know what that is, Simon." And she didn't. But the fear in his voice told her whatever it was, it certainly wasn't good.

"A poison that can be absorbed through the skin and ingested. It's still questionable whether the coroner will survive."

She bit her lip as her understanding of the fears he held took root. "I'll be careful. I promise, Simon. I'm sorry for snapping too."

He parked, but not before she noted a subtle change to the entry of the house. Ulrich sat at the front. "Simon. Ms Niamh."

"Is that necessary?" she asked once inside.

Simon turned. "I won't risk losing you, Niamh." He cupped her cheek. "I—"

"Niamh!" Finn rushed her, grabbing her in a bone-crushing hug.

Whatever Simon had been about to say, it was too late. She glanced over her brother's shoulder and watched as his face resumed its regular "everything is okay" mask.

The tide of excitement pulled her into the lounge.

Simon watched as Finn and Danny demanded Niamh's attention. He'd nearly spilled his guts right there in the hallway until Finn had come running in.

She deserved better, though. Hearts and flowers and a romantic dinner.

He shuffled into the kitchen and rattled in the freezer, looking for something to cook that would fill their hungry bellies, give them time to talk and catch up and keep his mind occupied.

He settled on steak. That he could grill. Salad was simple, and he tugged out the ingredients, dumping them into the sink to wash, then set about preparing it.

From time to time, laughter would spill out, and he'd smile. Niamh deserved to be happy.

A throat cleared in the doorway. The younger brother, Danny, stood there with an envelope in hand. "I'm not supposed to do this. Mam wrote it. Said there was someone who would need this, but not to open it straight away. Time wasn't right, and by reading it, things would change." He shrugged. "I don't get all this magic stuff and prophecies, but she was adamant. So here."

He passed the envelope to Simon and watched as he peered at it. "So when...?"

"Mam said at the moment of most despair. You'll know when, she assured me." Danny jigged from one foot to the other. "I want to say, Niamh has never been happier. She's the sort of sister who doesn't ask for anything but gives. She feels deep. You make her smile, and that's a rare thing. Keep treating her well and there'll be no trouble from me."

Simon didn't quite know what to say. "Oh. Well, thank you, I guess."

Danny leaned in. "But if you hurt her, I'll gut you like a fucking pig and cook you on a spit."

Now Simon hissed. "Okay, let's get one thing clear. Your sister and me? That's private. I won't hurt her, at least never intentionally. Second, you're in my house, so threaten me and you get the shittiest jobs I can come up with."

Danny guffawed. "I like you. You're no pushover."

"Great. Here's the steak. Take it out to the patio. I'll bring the rest soon."

He gathered the oil and equipment slowly, needing time to consider the interaction with Danny. The man was fiery and loud, but Finn was likely more dangerous, with the narrow-eyed glare when he thought no one was watching and the stealthy moves.

On a sigh, Simon gathered up the tray and entered the lounge on his way to the patio. "Niamh, if you could arrange drinks?"

She nodded and smiled, the look heating his insides. Probably always would, he thought, remembering back to comments his grandfather had made during his wooing of Marta.

When the drinks came, they gathered around, and Niamh took up position in a chair. "So, what the hell have you done to get yourselves banished?"

Silence descended.

*S*imon almost winced at her harsh question. *Almost.*

Finn growled something under his breath and shifted in his seat.

Danny looked at the ground, then back up again, feet shuffling. "We went to see the witch to find out exactly what happened that night when they banished you. We'd both had a little too much to drink. Finn told her he'd take her wand and shove it up her kazoo. Me? I... I lost my temper."

Niamh paled, her mouth tight. "I have to say, I'm shocked either of you would take part in such activities. You know the fairies of our glade owe fealty to the witch. She's protected us for generations, and you can't just demand—"

"They sent you away, Niamh! With no warning." Danny flung his hand out, agitated and angered. "It wasn't right! You did nothing wrong. She told me... She said there was a prophecy, and it was time-and-place stuff. I call bullshit on that, sis."

Finn rose and walked in a tense circle. "Aye. More than that, the elders came to the house when they thought we'd passed out. You're being sacrificed to appease some bloody god or being who said one day a girl must go forth and blah blah bullshit."

Simon waited for more, and when it didn't come, he interjected. "So, do you know the prophecy they speak of?"

Finn shook his head. "No. Once they realised I wasn't out of it, they had me pack, woke Danny, then hustled us into the car, headed for the airport."

Simon stared at the steaks and decided, "The fairies in the glade may know. We should ask them."

Niamh turned, speared him with a look. "Why?"

"Because what your brothers have just told us? There was a premeditation, Niamh. You deserve better than that."

Her gaze softened. "But I have better. I have you, and Finn and Danny. I love my new job."

"Niamh, I want you to have options and choices. To blindly accept—"

She moved closer, and the heat of her nearness scalded him. "I have exactly what I want. From the moment I met you, Simon, I knew. I was scared, yes. Did I act like a coward? Yes I did, but deep down I knew the truth: that you were the one I'd choose."

Finn sucked in a deep breath, and when Simon glanced over Niamh's shoulder, he caught sight of the shock on Danny's face.

"Niamh?" Finn's voice echoed in the silence.

"My choice, Finn. That's the way of fairies."

"But, Niamh…"

Simon blinked. "What is it you're telling me, Niamh?" He wasn't dumb, but there was more to the announcement than he could grasp.

"Fairies can choose a mate, to use your terminology. Any mate. Not all do. Many pair up in their younger days, and it's light-hearted fun. No serious entanglement. But a fairy can choose their partner for life too. That's what I'm doing, Simon. If you'll have me?"

He gulped, because she'd once more taken the forward step before he could find the words. It was humbling.

Framing her face with shaking hands, he tugged her closer. "My mate. Forever." He kissed her, softly, tenderly, and ensured she understood that this was a promise, a vow. One he'd keep.

Her hand slid to his chest, covered his heart, and warmth suffused him. The animal inside him stretched with pleasure.

CHAPTER 20

Niamh held the precious license in her hand. In the weeks that followed since Simon had urged her to get her learner's permit, he'd taken her out daily, arranged for lessons on her days off, and drilled her with facts to prepare her for today.

"You did well." Simon hugged her. "In the last few weeks, you've listened carefully, read all the information, and practiced. Now that you have your license, where would you like to go first?"

She'd readied herself for the question. "The glade."

He blinked. "The glade?"

"Yes. I want to see your animal, if you're okay with that. Then I want to put on my circlet and dance and be with you—all of you."

Simon nodded, his hair moving in the slight breeze. She knew he'd not gone there yet, too involved with the investigation into the abductions. There'd been another one earlier on in the week, and he'd ramped up his guards on her, but today, it was just them.

"When?"

"How about now?" She smiled and so did he, though his was strained. "Unless you have to do something else. I'll understand if you're busy." Niamh truly did. She'd watched the steady process of people he met with. Knew that from time to time, he also had to travel "off-site," as he called it, to meet with vampires.

"Actually, I have a meeting with Cressida and Xavier. I thought you might wish to come with me. We could do the glade tomorrow?"

She blinked. "Sure, but I should change, then. I mean, she's the overlord and all."

He smiled. "I'm sorry we can't go today. I arranged the meeting with her yesterday, as they've been sorting out the mess from the vampire scandal."

Niamh placed her finger against his lips. "I understand totally. You have responsibilities as the pack leader, and sometimes other things have to wait, but I know you will try to make time for me. Like this." She waved her hand. He'd taken the Friday afternoon off with her so she could take her test and offer moral support. One guard would have been okay, but to have him there? It bolstered her confidence.

He made to hand her the keys, but she shook her head. "No. You drive. Tomorrow, I'll drive for the first time on my license to the glade." She felt her wings do the funny happy wiggle and watched his face note that.

"Okay."

They climbed into the car, and she settled herself, pleased to relax. Since he'd announced he'd made her appointment, she'd been a mass of worry.

"Danny and Finn found a job with Amalia and Frank." His words were careful, and Niamh turned, surprised.

"What? When?"

Simon laughed. "Yesterday. They start Monday and said that as soon as they're able, they're going to find somewhere of their own to live. I told them they were welcome to stay, but Finn informed me they had no intentions of cramping our style. Or letting us cramp theirs."

Niamh frowned. "But they've just arrived and—"

"Niamh, sweetheart, they need their own place just as much as we do."

"But—"

"They won't be far away. I offered them a cottage between work and us. They're considering it. With them that close, we can be there if they need us. They're both planning on getting their learner's permits, and I've said I'll help them there too. They're grown men, Niamh, and need to learn to live their own lives and be self-sustaining."

Her face flamed, though not because he was telling her anything that was unexpected. She knew they were adults, but after the long months apart, she felt they needed to reconnect.

"I know they're grown-up. I just... It's hard. They worried about me after I left, and to be honest, they were always on my mind. It's like... We're connected, but during those months, the communication lines blurred. I want to fix that."

He pulled into the driveway. "Come on. It's not that bad. You'll see them most days, I would imagine. Besides, with those sexy wings..." Simon winked.

"I've already explained they're only good for a brief burst, like..." She blushed again, face burning.

The glow in his eyes turned wolfish. "I do like the way you flutter about in the throes of passion."

Niamh couldn't control the groan that escaped. She'd never live those saucy encounters down, she guessed.

Simon reached over, grazing his mouth over hers. "I know you 're scared to let them go again, but they need it as much as us. There's this human saying, 'If you love something, set it free. If it's meant to be, they'll return.' They'll come back. They love you too."

She hung her head. "I know."

Simon cupped her cheek. "I know the distance is too far for you to fly, but now you have your license and car. Soon they'll have theirs. And there's always your phone."

"I guess."

"Come on, let's go inside. You can shower and change, and I'll watch you. Ogle you. Have hot wicked thoughts about you." He jiggled his eyebrows suggestively, and she laughed.

"You're so bad! Who did you learn these things from?"

"Gramps!" He laughed, and she giggled, having electronically met Frederick in the last week, along with Marta.

"When are they coming to visit?"

"Three or four weeks. Depends on how soon they can get the kids sorted, find somewhere to stay, and Marta is over her morning sickness."

Taking Simon's hand, she tugged him to a stop at the door. "They could have stayed here."

"I offered it, Niamh, but he was insistent on a serviced apartment. Said the kids and everything else was too much for everyone right now. And to be honest, I'm not sure the kids wouldn't barge in while you're screaming in orgasm and your wings are glowing."

She slid a hand over her flushed face. "I'm not that bad."

"No, you're that good." He chuckled.

*S*imon pushed his concerns to the back of his mind. Tonight he'd meet with Cressida, the head vampire, and Xavier, the master of the House of Tudor nest and a councillor, and he'd be bringing Niamh with him.

Upon arriving at the large and imposing mansion, he gave his name at the guard post, taking a moment to check out the new processes. "How long has this been up?"

The guard said, "About two months. Since everything happened, the councillors and vamps have gotten a little uneasy."

Simon could well imagine. The losses of life the houses had experienced over the last couple years could have been catastrophic. It was careful management that had brought many back from the brink.

"You're good to go through now, sir."

The boom gate in front of the car lifted, and Simon started up the driveway.

"I didn't really pay that much attention to the vampire issues, but it seems to me that Attar victimised them?" Niamh spoke quietly.

"Yeah, he did a hell of a number on the vampire population. Humans of course, blamed all paranormals, as they do, because they fear our skills and abilities. Humans are fickle. Once Cressida's crew won, then things changed. Even though the popular support has swung back behind them, it's going to take years to undo the damage."

They drove up to the portico, and she glanced up. "What an impressive building."

"Isn't it? It's not the original house, though. That was burned down about twenty years ago. They moved in here after the fire and stayed. They're also one of the oldest American houses. Hope, the master's life partner, is the daughter of a previous *Yeux Secondes*. And David, Genevieve's mate? He's her brother and was also *Yeux Secondes* for a while."

"It all sounds very complicated."

"It is, and it isn't. Now come on, they'll be waiting for us inside."

They climbed from the car, and Simon took Niamh's arm. They headed up the stairs to the door, which slid open in silence.

Cressida, Daniel, Hope, and Xavier waited inside the hall, and introductions were made all around. He'd only met Daniel, Hope, and Xavier once, briefly, and now here he was making enquiries as to something that might smash the world of vampires once again.

"Please. Come into my office," Xavier urged, and they entered, settling on deep red cushions of the old chairs.

Cressida cleared her throat. "Xavier, Simon is here in an official capacity. He has requested information that normally would not be a matter of the public record."

Simon cleared his throat. "You may or not be aware of several humans being targeted and going missing in the last twelve months. We found many of their remains in the abandoned warehouse you own." He thrust an official photo across Xavier's desk.

"This is one of ours?" Xavier turned it over and checked the address on the back, then slid it to Hope.

"Yes, that's one of ours. Due for demolition and replacement with multiple-family dwellings." She tugged a small tablet from the table and input the date. "I believe the police raided it recently. That's what they found?"

Simon nodded. "Indeed. My man, Morrow—an investigator our pack has now employed—did some digging. Your man Simeon Caldwell leased it to an Albert Persible."

Hope's fingers flashed across the screen. "That's odd," she said, then showed the details to Xavier before sliding it across the desk for Simon to view. He showed Niamh.

"You have no lease on file. That is odd," Simon growled. "Is there some way you can—"

"Just a moment," Hope said, and her fingers moved, the rapid *tap tap tap* filling the silence. She looked up and frowned. "The file's been scrubbed. Badly, but still."

Simon leaned forwards. "Can you tell who or when—"

"Not me." Hope shook her head. "One moment, though, and I'll get our IT guys on it. They'll know more." She stood and moved away from the table, mobile phone in hand.

"What else do you need to know?" Xavier's face darkened as if he took responsibility for this breach.

"If Caldwell and Persible are working together, there will be other sites," Simon replied. "More leases. We humbly request that the files —or at least addresses—for any properties, especially those in the last six to eight weeks, that Caldwell had anything to do with be released to us. It is our belief that Persible is the one behind all this. We don't yet know how his connection to Caldwell happened, only that he's a prime suspect."

Cressida moved in her seat. "Why not hand this over to the Liaison Division?"

"He made a play for Niamh. Twice."

All eyes in the room swivelled to Niamh, who tried very hard to appear invisible and failed.

"But still," Daniel murmured.

"We've been closely watching the way your houses have autonomy to deal with judicial issues. We wish to achieve that same standing. To do so, we need to bring something to the table. Something with substance. Persible fits the bill."

"But he's human," Cressida added.

Simon shrugged. "We don't yet know that. What impacts the case further is that he treated the bodies discovered at the site with thallium. The coroner is expected to survive."

Hope returned to the table. "The team is looking into it right now. They'll also pull any file Persible has touched in the last three months, even if they're hidden or he's simply opened it." She tapped her long fingers against her ruby red lips. "He's so far down the pecking order, though, that he shouldn't be able to complete any kind of agreement without a supervisor signing off."

"There could be someone else?" Xavier asked.

"Perhaps." Hope lowered herself to the seat beside Xavier. "If there is, our people will find the connection."

"I'm going to ask Cressida, but if we wished to formalise an alliance between this pack and your houses, would you be amenable?" Simon pinned the blond woman with a stare.

"I see no reason not to be, but it would be a matter for the Council to determine, ultimately."

"Good. I'll make a formal request in the next week. It might be my second, Jessica, who follows it through, though, with your permission."

"Of course. We would welcome it," she answered.

With the initial business concluded, Hope rang for refreshments.

CHAPTER 21

$\mathcal{N}$ow he knew where the girl had gone. She was keeping company with a were—the Lord of Lycans, no less!

"Julien, you're totally sure this is where she is?"

"Oh, absolutely. I don't know what she is just yet, but there're whispers of wings. Perhaps she's a dragon shifter? I don't know. It doesn't matter. This'll screw with Genevieve's head, and that's all that matters to me. She and that upstart."

The third man shifted uncomfortably in his chair. "I don't really want to know. I'm doing you the favour, just as instructed by the Middle Man, okay? He owns my debt, and this finishes it," Simeon Caldwell whimpered.

"And you cleared your name from all the records as instructed?" Julien Delacorte demanded.

Caldwell bobbed his head in furious agreement. "Yes. I followed your instructions exactly as you gave them, Julien."

"Good." He smiled, and it was feral. Simeon quaked before him, and Julien turned to Albert. "You have your latest victim. Have at him."

He turned away and Albert sprang, injecting something into the human's neck.

"We're going to have so much fun, friend. Thank you for the lease, but it's time for your internal inspection of my playroom to begin." Albert's voice rose in a cadence of glee while Simeon's eyes closed... though not yet for the last time.

CHAPTER 22

Simon urged Niamh to guide the car beneath the canopy of trees, as she sighed. The meeting with the vampires the night before had been exhausting, but she'd kept going. It would have been difficult, unused to the interaction with the vampires, but he was proud of her, and he'd insisted that afterward they'd visit the glade.

Simon had already contacted the leader of the herd, and they'd assured him that their elders would be there.

"Thank you, Simon," she whispered, turning off the engine.

"What for? I promised we'd come."

She slid her hand over his cheek. "You did, but there's so many conflicting priorities right now. I mean, Morrow and the investigation, and—"

Simon shook his head. "No. You're my number one priority, Niamh. You always will be. Now come on, and bring that circlet. I want to see you dance again."

Niamh giggled as she scooped it up from the back seat of the car, then passed Simon the keys, given she had nowhere to secret them in her gown.

They entered the woods hand in hand, and the farther they went, the lighter her spirits became.

Stepping into the glade, Niamh gazed at the pretty flowers that had bloomed.

"Welcome, Lord of Lycans," an elderly voice called, and they turned as one, bodies already finely attuned after mere weeks together.

"I bid you good day, crone, and seek your memories." Simon bowed low.

"Then come. Sit with me on the rock and learn all you will." The older woman beckoned them both forwards. They took up the positions shown and waited. "You have questions about a prophecy, I understand. Let me see what I can tell you. Tell me what you know."

Niamh opened her mouth, but Simon shook his head. "They banished Niamh from her home. A witch lives in that glade. She cast runes upon the ground, and in haste, Niamh brushed against them."

The old woman's face tightened. "A witch? Esmerelda?"

Niamh nodded.

"Oh, child. Your journey from this point is perilous. I was there when the prophecy came about. Esmerelda—the witch—is a battle axe and a stickler for protocols. It predisposes you to clumsiness." The old woman's eyes clouded over, mists of blue, pink, and green whirling over the orbs of her eyes. *One day a child will be born. She'll be bonny and kind but her path difficult. She'll brush the runes of tomorrow, and banishment must follow. In the new place, love will grow and flourish, but evil awaits, the danger extreme. Only genuine love will find the path to her restoration.*"

Niamh cleared her throat. "Um, until the end, it's oddly specific."

The woman nodded. "The first is written, but the ending depends on those who seek the truth."

Simon cleared his throat, though his stomach churned. "I have one other question. About a mating between fairy and were... a wolf shifter."

The woman smiled. "That too is written. That the two shall meet and eventually, overcoming all trials, become one." She sighed. "Personally, I have never seen that come to pass, but if it's written, then someday... who knows? Well, I know only that if you're meant to be, the gods will ensure that happens." She rose. "I am weary of talking. We have promised you the glade and peace. It's yours. Be well." She shuffled away, leaving the pair alone.

Niamh glanced at him. "I don't know that it feels so celebratory right now," she whispered.

"Then we make our own. Tell me, Niamh, have you ever seen a shift?"

She shook her head, and he dragged her close. "The animal inside is close to the surface today. When you take wing, watch and I'll release him for a short while."

"Are you sure? I mean, what if someone is watching?"

He smiled. "No one is. I can smell the air, Niamh. The animal grants me the ability to smell strongly. But tell me something in response. As a shifter, the women can only conceive with their allotted mate. Some will take multiples, but the ritual is observed and only during the female's fertile cycle."

Niamh blushed and looked around. "You're sure no one is here?" They rarely spoke of the story of procreation, and never to outsiders.

Simon nodded.

She took his hands and dragged him to the very centre of the glade. Above them, the canopy soared. "When a fairy and her love decide they wish to procreate, they dance to the top of the trees. There, we find a sacred fruit, and if both partake, the graces bless their next loving. But the loving must happen here, in the centre of the glade, in this spot." She pointed to a bed of luxuriant flowers. "Every glade is slightly different, but the way remains the same. 'As it has been for centuries, so shall it be,'" she whispered.

"Would you share that fruit with me, Niamh?"

Her gaze captured his. "I would. When the time is right, Simon. But you're not a fairy, and I don't know if we can." Tears glazed her eyes.

He folded her close, seeing the dimming of her wings and the way the beating slowed. "If we can, one day, we'll find a way."

She nodded. "One day." But her voice remained low.

This wasn't quite what he planned. On a deep breath, he stepped back. "Take wing, Niamh, then watch."

The beating of her wings increased, and she rose, feet and body loose, the gown hugging curves he delighted in. Never releasing her gaze, Simon disrobed.

Her face shone, the movement of her wings speeding up as he exposed more flesh. Finally, naked, he watched her, his body tight with carnal hunger.

Then he released the wolf.

*N*iamh gasped. One moment a naked Simon stood there, and the next a very large white wolf replaced him.

With care, she floated towards the ground. He circled her, gazing deeply into her eyes. "Simon?"

The wolf bowed its head.

"Can I... can I touch you?"

He prowled closer, and she reached out, carefully letting her fingertips find the ends of his pelt before growing bolder, sinking them deep. "So soft," she muttered. Sliding to her knees before him, she gazed upon the creature. "So strong." Indeed he was, with thick sinewy haunches and a deep barrelled chest.

"Absolutely magnificent," she whispered, then gave a tiny laugh when his tongue darted out and licked her hand. He pawed the air until she took his... arm? Hand? Paw? She couldn't quite decide in her mind which it really was.

The wolf backed up and lifted his head, giving a single quiet growl. Before she could speak, Simon had returned.

"You understood me, didn't you? I mean, the wolf did..."

"We do. He and I both will protect you, Niamh. We—" He coughed and sighed. "I love you."

She teared up. "And I love you as well, Simon. You give me joy and peace. Love and such happiness."

She moved into his arms, and the kiss they shared was deep. Earthy.

"I want you, Niamh. Here, on this bed of flowers."

"But..."

"You don't want to?" he teased.

"I do, but the fruit... We're not really ready yet."

Simon shook his head. "Not yet, but we can practice."

With a nod, she reached for the shoulders of her gown and slid it down, noting his surprise when he realised she was naked beneath it. "Last time, you were..."

Niamh smiled and nodded. "Oh yes. And really turned on by you, even then."

He growled and hauled her close so their bodies touched.

The jutting of his cock at her belly was welcome, her breasts tingling with the awareness that soon he'd be sharing her body.

"Simon? Love me."

"I already do and always will." This time the kiss was tender, his hands roaming down her flanks, grasping her butt before rising to the ridges of her wings.

He touched them, and stars exploded in her mind. He'd learned that this was an erogenous zone, that when he touched and stroked, it was as if he were massaging the secret spot inside her body.

"I'm going to kiss your wings, then suck your breasts, Niamh. They're perfect. Just like you. And when you're so excited and hot, dripping wet for me, I'm going to fill your body with mine."

"Oh, Simon," she moaned, feeling the play of fingertips at the juncture of her wings. Her nipples were hard pebbles of need.

When he moved behind her, his mouth sliding oh so gently over the membranes while his hands cupped her breasts and tweaked her nipples, her legs almost gave way.

Her hands moved, wanting to rub over him, capture his engorged length and play with the sack that hung between his legs.

"Dear... gods," she cried as the first wave of orgasm hit, burying her so the only things that existed were him and her. "Please, Simon. Come to me."

He prowled, a hunter intent on capturing her. Loving her. Filling her.

She rose, and he took her shoulders while her legs twined around him.

When he slid deep, they both groaned with completion, and the sensual dance began.

They rose higher as she undulated and slid beneath him. He grunted, pushing deeper and faster, bodies entwined until the explosion sealed their pleasure.

When they finally stilled, they'd floated down and lay among the flowers.

Her eyes widened. "Um, Simon?"

He laughed. "I told you so."

"Niamh!" Simon bellowed. "Have you seen my suit coat?"

She slid out of the bathroom, toothbrush in hand. "I sent it off to be dry-cleaned. Jessica told me that's what you usually do. Otherwise, I would have cleaned it myself."

"Oh. Damn."

"Is that a problem?"

"I'm meeting Morrow this morning at the Liaison Division. I was planning to take it, so I looked the part."

Niamh's eyes glinted. "You always look the part. Just wear a shirt and tie, if you need something. Put on your leather trench coat and everyone will fall at your feet."

"Huh. You wearing that to work?"

He pointed to the minuscule bra and panty set he'd bought her, along with dozens of others.

"I was. Under my work clothes." She grinned. "Danny and Finn move out today, so tonight we celebrate."

Her wings flittered, and he grinned. "I'm glad you'll have something else on. Otherwise, I'd have to add to your guards."

Her face fell. "About that. Dr Arnett is getting a little upset about having armed men in the waiting room every day. I don't suppose you could—"

"Don't ask that of me, Niamh. I don't even like you driving yourself to work alone at this point."

She bit her lip. "But nothing has happened."

"Except Caldwell has disappeared."

"Simon, it's likely a coincidence. Morrow told you he's narrowing down all the spots. No one will make a play for me here, in a village that's basically controlled by your people."

He had no intention of telling her the extra precautions he'd taken with her safety. Including the tracker he'd placed in her car and the other in her bag.

"All right, for a little longer," Niamh agreed.

"Until we find him," Simon corrected. He knew she was chafing at the restrictions, and he couldn't really blame her, but his gut said soon there'd be another attempt. There was no way he'd let the psycho have her. She was too precious and important to him.

Their future lay ahead. Together.

She disappeared into the walk-in closet and appeared ten minutes later in a skirt and blouse, her nude pumps matching the tiny bag she'd taken to using. That Niamh wore no make-up pleased him no end. Her beauty shone through with no cosmetics and potions.

"I'm heading out now. It's Lisa's last day, and I need to set up the cake I'm collecting from Amalia's. Dr Arnett is providing the morning tea too. We're going to close for an hour between ten and eleven, and we've actually been able to keep the appointment slots clear."

He tugged her close, kissing her, luxuriating for a moment in the feel of her curves against his body. "Have a good day. I'll see you tonight. I love you."

"I love you too, you sexy wolf. Now I better get moving."

He watched as she scurried from the room, then turned and started dressing.

*N*iamh entered Amalia's in a great mood. "Thanks for doing this," she called as the woman slid the cake across the counter.

"Our pleasure. Lisa's great, but I reckon you'll give her a run for her money in the bedside manner department."

Niamh laughed and waved, turning to the door. She heard the bell dinging as it closed behind her and she hurried to her car. She'd just opened it and set the cake inside when the hairs on her nape rose.

Spinning, she caught sight of a large man, his coat black and his eyes wide.

"So, my precious, I finally have you in my clutches."

He slid a sharp implement against her neck.

She felt the prick, and darkness descended.

But not before she dropped her phone to the road.

Niamh was unconscious by the time he bundled her into her little car and drove away.

CHAPTER 23

Simon was driving on the highway when his mobile phone rang.

"Hey, Simon? What time is Niamh due to arrive at work?" Dr Arnett's voice echoed on the line.

The sudden sickening ice that formed in his gut told him it had all gone wrong.

"She was heading to Amalia's, collecting the cake, and then going directly to the clinic. She didn't make it?"

"Oh... no. I've tried her cell, but it rings out. Perhaps... Can you try?"

He glanced at the freeway. Cars jammed end to end, but an exit lay just ahead. He made his way in that direction as intuition told him she needed him. Now.

"I'll do that, but I'm on my way. If she turns up, tell her to call me." In his heart, though, he feared the worst.

He disconnected and tried her number. It rang out. He tried a second time and cursed, slamming his hand against the steering wheel when it went to voicemail.

He cut through multiple lanes towards the exit while horns blared the drivers' displeasure, sweating even as his body chilled.

Niamh. Her name became a chant in his mind.

He scrolled through his contacts list and found Ulrich's number. "Where the fuck is Niamh?" he bellowed once the call connected.

"We don't know. I'm sending Bailey to check at Amalia's in case she broke down. But, boss? I don't think that's the case."

Hell, Simon knew it wasn't. But his blood pressure was spiking off the charts as terror crowded his mind. "Check the tracking on her car and her bag. Maybe there's been an accident."

"I'll get right on it, boss, and I'll call you back."

It would take the best part of an hour for him to get back home. "Damn it."

On a whim, he contacted James Morrow. When the call connected, he demanded, "Where the fuck is Persible?"

"I've literally just received the list. Why?"

"Because I think he has Niamh. How long will it take you to—"

"Wait. Niamh? Didn't he try for her before?"

"Yes. But she's missing." He refused to consider where she might be and in what state. He had to focus on the hopes that she'd be all right.

"I'm on my way. I'll have my men deployed as quickly as I can."

Simon wanted to point out that it likely wouldn't be soon enough but bit it off. No matter the steps he'd taken to safeguard Niamh, they hadn't been enough. And that burned him.

*N*iamh came to, feeling as if she were fighting through a black haze.

"What happened?"

The sound of an engine filled her awareness, but it was dark, as if she were in a cave or hidden from the sun.

Terror filled her, and she felt the quickening of her breath. The jitters in her nerves.

A sense of self-protection rose. *Stay calm.* It wasn't easy, but she made her fingers search and felt the short stubby hairs of carpet. She was in a small place, barely big enough to contain her. Her legs bent up with the lack of space.

Wherever she was, it wasn't stable, as she rolled slightly.

"Oomph," she cried as her head connected with something metallic and awareness fled again.

Simon struggled to find his equilibrium. *Where is she?*

He drove to the street where she'd stopped to pick up the cake and found Ulrich waiting in his car, his face grim.

"Boss? I found her phone." He handed over the device.

Now the fears threatened to swamp Simon. She had no phone, and he knew she wouldn't throw it away. It was her lifeline to Finn and Danny. And him.

"Have you located her yet?"

Ulrich's face paled. "We found a location for her trackers. Thrown from a window on the highway. Whoever took her found them, got rid of them. We have no straightforward way to track her down. Boss... I'm sorry. I should have trailed her. Her car was found dumped in the next town."

Ulrich's words came from far away as Simon stared ahead. Beyond. "This isn't your mistake or mine. Persible is dangerous, and we allowed her to go without an escort. I should have insisted, but she needed her freedom. The only thing we can hope is she's about to get away. She can't fly far, but surely..."

It wasn't much, but he'd hold on to that hope for as long as he could. She was bright. Smart. She'd find a way.

Anything else just wasn't acceptable.

His phone blared. "Morrow, what have you found out?"

"Nothing good. There are five locations. We need to check each, because they're in remote areas. I'm on my way to your office. I'll be there in fifteen minutes with the coordinates of the locations."

Simon hung up and turned to Ulrich. "My office. Now."

They moved with careful grace, muscles rippling with frustration, aware of the dangers, as they'd seen Persible's handiwork on the roof of the warehouse. They knew what he was capable of. At this stage, the only positive was he hadn't had her long enough to do much. But time would run out, and Simon had to find her before that occurred.

CHAPTER 24

*A*lbert Persible settled his latest treasure into the cage he'd prepared for her.

"What a shame. They were so careful until now. Now you're mine, and I intend to enjoy you. But first I must recreate my other toy to perfection."

The man on the rack, naked and bleating, excited him.

With a deep inhalation, he considered his tools. Julien had ensured he had what he required. He'd taken great care when vetting the location for Persible, and he was grateful and frustrated in equal turns.

Once again, Albert checked the bonds he'd installed on the table. Julien hadn't batted an eye at his request for a mortuary table. It was one of Albert's most prized items, and it pleased him that he'd been able to bring it with him. He hadn't hidden it in the warehouse, but clearing out his existing lair allowed him to declutter his collection.

His gaze settled on the collection of knives and steels.

"Which one, Caldwell? What do you think?" He hefted a large knife, and the man cleared his bowels on the table. "Oh, dear, that's not the way to begin, is it?"

Persible was a stickler and sighed, replacing the knife. "Now I will cleanse you." The large hose he'd purchased at a firehouse auction had seen much use in the cleaning process.

He turned it on the man squirming on the table. "There now. Much better, isn't it?"

Caldwell coughed and spluttered as if he were drowning, and with a heavy sigh, Persible released his hands so the man could sit up and clear his airway. "Dear me, so dramatic. Come now, lie back and rest. We're about to play, and I don't like interruptions."

When the man lay back, Persible once again grabbed the flailing hands and refastened the bond. "Now, let's begin, shall we?"

Simon and Morrow searched through the short list of locations. The House of Tudor had purchased several properties in the mountainous region just south of the township where he lived.

Each was remote and difficult to reach.

Checking the real estate listings for them, he noted them described as perfect hideaways with multiple buildings on-site. Secluded. "Fuck it all!"

Looking closer, he noted that several of them were in areas with limited cell range. That would make coordinating rescue attempts more problematic.

With every passing moment, Simon knew Niamh's time ran short.

"Get me a layout of the properties. We can't send drones over in case they tip him off, so we need whatever is available from the cities before we can move in."

His cell beeped, and he picked up. "What?" he barked.

"Simon?" Frederick's voice came down the line. "What's wrong?"

Simon hissed a breath, knowing intimately now, how alarmed Frederick would be learning Niamh was missing. Frederick would worry about him too. He'd seen enough of what Frederick went through when his grandmother died and had thought he'd understood before, but now that faded into insignificance beside the tearing pain he endured. "Niamh. They've taken her."

"We'll be on our way within the hour."

Simon couldn't summon the energy to say no. His grandfather had never failed to support him, and it appeared he wouldn't this time either. "Thank you."

He hung up, his brain a whirl of ideas, but nothing made sense. He turned blind eyes towards Jessica when she arrived. "I heard. Give me a list of the addresses. I'll send in our people. They'll find her quickly."

Simon didn't respond, and she came close, tugging him into a hug. "We're shifters, Simon. They'll smell her out."

He blinked. "They're going to need clothes, then." He choked the words out, realising just how mindless he must appear.

Jessica cupped his cheeks, her eyes damp. "We'll find her, Simon. We'll get her back. You hang in there."

The screaming stopped, and Niamh shook. It had been horrific, the sounds and emotions overwhelming, until she'd finally passed out in sympathy.

She stayed determinedly away from the edges of the cage, keeping her eyes closed and her entire body turned in the other direction. The scent was enough to turn her stomach.

But the sounds, they gave her an idea of what had taken place. She didn't want to see, because that would show her what her future would be. Too terrifying to accept.

"Come on, pretty toy. Look at the masterpiece I've made."

She was chilled to the bone, and horror and revulsion fought for uppermost control of her mind. He knew she was awake. She set her body, refusing to look.

"Suit yourself, my dear. It will be your turn soon enough."

All Niamh could think was "Where are you, Simon?" But she feared he'd arrive too late.

lbert cackled as he photographed his latest work. It truly was a masterpiece, every section perfectly prepared. "Too bad you don't wish to see. But one day, the world will be ready, and my life's work will find acceptance."

He glanced at the fairy in the cage. *A fairy! Who'd have thought it?* He'd never held such a paranormal before, usually choosing those who served so he might give them their moment to shine. But now, considering, he wondered if he'd done himself a disservice.

Those wings! Magnificent. They'd sparkled with shades of pink and orange when he'd taken her. Now they were a dull green.

"Changeable."

He wondered what they'd look like when separated from the body. Would they turn black like onyx or an ashy grey? He couldn't wait to investigate that. This was going to be an adventure, and he couldn't help himself, snapping photos of the drooping membranes where she remained huddled behind the bars.

"Don't pout little one. Your turn is coming soon. And then, everyone will know the name of Albert Persible. Master of Art."

She whimpered and huddled even further down.

With a sigh, he turned back to the remains of Caldwell. Now they just felt... mundane. Ordinary. Ah, well, tomorrow he'd start his new project. "Best I clean up, then."

But not before he treated his pieces with the special product, he thought with glee.

Sliding on his mask and gloves, he surveyed what remained, then reached for the additive he favoured and began.

CHAPTER 25

Night fell, and the vampires came to call. Simon met Daniel and Cressida in his office.

"We cannot imagine the unspeakable pain you must feel, Simon. Please, how can we assist?" Cressida asked.

He glanced at the blond woman, who perched on the seat across from his desk. "I don't..." He paused, his brain aching from the long hours spent poring over records, taking calls, and setting up teams.

Jessica hovered at his shoulder. "We're sending teams in the morning to search the locations we've shortlisted. We can't send them tonight as we don't yet have the details—"

"What do you need?" Daniel sat forwards earnestly in his seat.

"The city is blocking our access to the planning records for the properties we've requested," Simon answered, exhaustion dragging at him. He raised bleary eyes. "We think we can get a court order first thing in the morning."

Cressida glanced at Daniel, then back at Simon. "Give us the details you require. We'll make it happen."

He nodded, and Jessica gathered a sheaf of papers and turned for the copier. "I'll have it in a moment."

Cressida's hands closed over his. "You've been a good friend to the vampires, Simon. The pack has always been there when we've needed help. What makes this worse is that these secrets have come from our own." Her eyes glittered coldly. If he'd been able, he might have shuddered at her fury. Right now, he was too overwhelmed by Niamh's absence. "We will correct these mistakes. It will never happen again under my watch."

With burning eyes, he surveyed the two vampires, aware she meant every word she uttered. It wasn't any real comfort to him, though.

Niamh was still out there, in the clutches of Albert Persible. In danger.

The smile he gave them was probably lopsided, but right now, Simon didn't care. "Thank you." He meant it, even as his hands curled into fists.

"We will take our leave now," Cressida whispered.

They rose and spoke with Jessica, gathering contact details so they might send their findings through quickly.

Remaining at his desk, eyes on his computer, he didn't acknowledge their leaving. His mind felt disconnected and remote, as if it searched for Niamh's essence. If they could gain the information they needed, they'd be able to go forth, seek her out first thing in the morning.

Simon could only hope Niamh still had time. Anything else was crushing.

*N*iamh's scream rent the night, a howl of pain and terror.

The man before her grinned. "Interesting." He stalked around her in a wide circle, inspecting his handiwork. Membranes stretched to their full extent, even torn a little as desperation filled her.

"Let me go! Please."

Muscles in her back stretched taut as she fought against the instinctive need to take wing. To do that would tear the now ragged edges of her wings. Grey edged into her vision.

"No! No sleep!" His hand shot out, slapping her hard as tears streamed from aching eyes down her cold cheeks.

"Let me go," she whispered. "Have mercy."

His eyes glittered in the artificial lights of the basement room. If she turned her head, she'd see the cage where he'd kept her. Smell the stink of her own fear.

"I'm making you into artwork, precious. Can't you see that?" His voice rang with a sing-song cadence, and she knew he was mad. Noted it in the tight way his face settled the whole time he gazed at her.

He'd attached her to the table, wings pinned with large metal hooks, bound at hand and foot. Then, with a razor-sharp knife, he'd removed her clothes, slicing them to long ribbons with an "ah" of satisfaction.

"Now tell me, does this hurt?" His hand whipped out and tugged at the edges of her wing, and she howled again, terror uppermost in her mind. The darkness settled again, and she welcomed the relief, but not before she heard him curse.

Simon sat before the computer. He'd not slept. How could he? Niamh must have been terrified. Perhaps already in pain or... dead.

It wasn't yet sunrise, but the hours of night had ticked away slowly. Every frantic beat of his heart willed the morning to begin so he might send his people out. Looking for her. Before him lay a pile of her clothing. His people would each sniff, then go out. It was all he could do. So very little.

His gut roiled, and he rubbed his knuckles against his eyes, trying vainly to hold back the scorching tears that pricked in the abused orbs.

A car pulled up. He barely had the energy to stand, but he did so anyway. Niamh needed him to be strong.

Murmuring came from the front door. Then his office door

slammed open and Frederick came in, followed by Marta. The children weren't in sight, but Simon guessed the sleeping youngsters being carried inside by helping hands.

Jessica hovered by the doorway, her own face pale and drawn. He knew Finn and Danny were pacing the length of the house, nearly as distressed as he at Niamh's absence.

"Damn it. You still haven't found her?" Frederick's rough growl echoed in the silence.

"No."

"What have you found out?" Marta enfolded Simon in a hug, and he let the reassurance seep into his chilled bones.

"The vamps have secured an emergency order to gain access to the records." He laughed bitterly. "They roused the city manager, who called his people in. They're searching their records now."

"You always had a good relationship with the vamps. It's good you're working together," Frederick offered. "How soon do they think they'll have the information?"

"Some records were archived, but they were retrieving them—" Simon glanced to his watch. "—an hour ago. Cressida nominated one of our new pack members, David, to attend, and he'll send the information through as soon as he has it. The vamps had to head back to their houses. It'll be dawn soon. So we won't be able to count on them again, until night falls."

"That's another full day. Time for Persible to continue his 'work.'" Frederick air-bracketed the word.

That was what he feared. "We have to find her soon, Gramps."

"We will, son. Soon."

CHAPTER 26

"Simon? We have the plans." David's voice filtered down the line.

"You've got them? Everything?"

"We have everything that's on file. I'm looking through them quickly." In the distance, Simon could hear the sounds of a car moving at speed. "Genevieve is driving while I check them. You should look them over, but there's two in particular that could be where he has her. One has a basement, buried deep, which is likely soundproofed against neighbours, though there aren't any for at least two miles in any direction. The other has a remote cabin, but it's nearer the road."

"How soon can you be here? I can have the pack hunters massed in an hour." He glanced up. Jessica was already nodding and sprinting for the phone.

He detested that they hadn't just been able to hit every property, but he'd accepted—unwillingly—the advice that to do so would undo the hard work and leaps they'd taken towards proving themselves capable of policing the pack. Of handling their own judicial processes without intervention from the humans.

"I can be there in about twenty minutes."

He hung up and scrubbed his hands over his face, feeling the rasp of the day's growth under his fingers.

"Hang in there, Niamh. We're coming for you."

Nearly forty-eight hours had passed since her abduction. Long hazy hours of self-recrimination and string pulling. Hours begging and pleading with the gods.

Rapping at the front door had him sitting upright.

This time, it wasn't Frederick who opened the door, and shock ricocheted through Simon as the elder fairy stepped inside the office. "I told you of the prophecy, Lord of Lycans. I can offer no wisdom as to where she is, but we feel her pain. Acutely." The woman pushed the heel of her hand against her chest. "In accord, we stand beside you this day." Her face greyed. "All I know is she is in great pain."

"How do you—" He had to swallow the lump obscuring his throat. "How do you know that?"

The elder smiled bitterly. "I am the keeper of lore. The knower of secrets. I feel on the wind and knew of yours and her twin pain. Find her, Lord, before it's too late, for the evil has already touched her."

Bile rose now, coating the inside of his mouth. "I—" Simon cleared his throat. "We'll find her. We have a plan, and the pack hunters are massing even as we speak."

The roar of bikes and cars arriving filled the air.

The elder fairy nodded. "Then I should leave you."

Without thinking, he reached out. "Stay. She may need you. I've already called in Dr Arnett to treat her too, just in case."

"All wise precautions," the elder stated. "I shall stay, then. Your grandfather is here. I will go out to him. Offer support to the two fairies I feel are also here."

"Finn and Danny. Niamh's brothers," Simon choked out.

She rose. "I can't tell you all will be well. I cannot know that, but I see true love. That is the deciding factor, according to the prophecy."

*S*imon had gathered the pack hunters, all chosen for speed, fighting ability, and their tracking skills. He'd need all that and more to find Niamh. Morrow, Frederick, Ulrich, and Bailey had also joined the group, ready to help in whatever capacity necessary.

As he spoke with the group, he heard two sets of footsteps outside. "Please come in," Simon called out.

David walked through the back door, files in his hands, Genevieve just behind him. They joined the others around the large table in the centre of the room.

"I've narrowed it down, as I told you." David placed each file down carefully, and one by one peeled back the folder cover so they could see the plans that lay below. "These are the layouts of the properties themselves. You'll see they're remote." He placed them side by side so the heads of the teams Simon had worked out could peer at them from beside him.

"These are the house and building plans." He laid them over each property guide so they could get an idea of what the infrastructure was. "These two"—he pointed to two he'd placed side by side—"are the ones I would think are the most logical locations."

"To be honest, I agree with David," Genevieve stated. "They're far enough away from any other buildings that no one will hear. He'll have somewhere to stash remains until he's ready to place them out. We know he likes to age them before he takes them to his chosen storage location." Her eyes glinted with fury. "He also treats them with thallium, so if anyone finds them, do. Not. Touch. Make note of the location, report it back, but do not, at all costs, touch the remains." She cut her glare to the leaders of the hunting teams.

They nodded in silence, fully aware of the dangers, as Dr Arnett had already been through the litany of damage to the coroner.

"I've also got the lieutenant on standby," she continued. "He'll send teams in as soon as we have Niamh. I'm sorry, my lord, but it's the best I can do. We cannot allow you to prosecute this internally as there are too many para species involved."

Simon could hear the sorrow in her words. "I understand, Genevieve. I thank you for your work with the Liaison Division."

His gaze shifted back to the plans. "We can send larger contingents to the two properties, smaller ones scoping out the others."

Morrow nodded. "I agree with David's conclusions. These are the most logical. You're going to need electronics people on hand too. We don't expect booby traps—he's far too focused on his work—but we still need to be aware and alert." He leaned in. "This one, though, this is the one I'd think. The basement is fully contained. It has bathing and waste facilities already in place. The other he'd need to jury-rig, and I'm not sure he's that kind of planner."

Genevieve's eyes narrowed. "You're a profiler?"

Morrow glanced up, his face tight. "I'm many things. Lived a long time and done much."

Simon didn't much care about the answer right now. He just wanted Niamh back. With a whirl, he faced Ulrich and Bailey. "You two will come with me. We'll go to the basement facility with Jamison."

"You should station the doctor at a location central to both locations. That way she can get to either within minutes," Frederick interjected, and Simon grunted his agreement.

"We need to move fast," he growled. Once they were within a mile, they'd leave the cars, shift to cover the distance as quickly as possible, then shift back prior to storming the locations.

They'd already handed out supplies. Satellite phones Jessica had laid her hands on quickly, emergency first aid supplies, and handheld radios so they could contact those who'd remain with the vehicles.

Without another word, they moved into their groups and headed for the cars. No one needed to say it, but time was running out.

Niamh couldn't gasp or moan, the rictus of pain from her back stealing any form of utterance. All she wanted was

Simon. But he hadn't come, and now the maniac had done the unthinkable.

Simon. Right now, she couldn't bring his visage to her mind, because the blackness she so dearly wished for danced at the edges of her awareness.

Her wings, severed, were pinned to a wall opposite her.

"See how they turn black? Beautiful. A true gem." The man she now knew to be Albert Persible, fairly danced with glee. "I'll let you rest a while, and then we can begin." He rubbed his hands together as he captured her gaze.

She wanted to shrink away from the look on his face, but fighting against the bonds was impossible, the ropes too tight to do anything other than abrade and cut at her flesh, as she'd already painfully learned.

Her gut seized, and bile wanted to rise in her stomach. Not that anything remained in it. She'd vomited the last of the contents when he'd begun sawing, and he'd hosed down the surface where she rested, her face lying against the tabletop. She could detect the faint coppery stink of his past victims, knew this was where many had met their ends.

She wondered if they were watching, haunting this evil place. The thought followed her down the dark tunnel to oblivion.

The bike's engine howled at being pushed. Simon didn't care, because it brought him closer to Niamh. With each passing second, the danger to her grew more acute.

The other bikes around him, both ahead and behind, would protect the Lord of Lycans; his own personal guards—normally unrequired—would flank him. The team led by the hulking Jamison would assess the situation, then strike hard while seeking to shield Niamh. Simon would only be allowed to enter once they could categorically call the site clear.

Jamison's bike came to a halt, his hand raised. Dust and debris flew up, and Simon dragged his dirt bike to a halt beside the big man.

"From here on in, we go by foot. Sanderson, you take the first aid equipment. Lincoln, you've got the phone. Jervis, the handhelds. You know the drill. Circle, let me check. Once I give the signal, every window and door are an access point. Teams of three. The basement is our preferred location. If the lady is there, protect at all costs. She is the lord's future mate."

No other words were necessary. He felt their reassurance and compassion. They knew what it cost him. The sense of camaraderie was thick.

They moved from the bikes, two cars coming to a halt beside them. Ulrich and Bailey climbed from one. "Not too late, are we?"

Simon shook his head.

Morrow climbed from his car. "I'll wait here. When you find her, if you need medical attention, I'll escort Dr Arnett up."

Jamison nodded. "Come on now, boys. Let's go."

They stripped quickly, stashing clothes into small bags they would carry in their mouths. Magic flashed, the muscles, bones, and sinews growing and reforming in an instant. Then they moved, legs flying, muzzles wide open, seeking the scent of Niamh that they'd all experienced back at Simon's house.

Undergrowth caught at the hair covering his body.

The pack ran fast, eating up the ground, and within minutes they had circled the house.

The log cabin mansion rose in the centre of a clearing. A curl of smoke rose, and there, the tang of decay. His head moved to the side, and he padded towards a sack. Another scent, acrid, had him backing away.

He was the last to flash back to human form, dressing quickly, his black pants and shirt blending into the tree line. "Over there," he whispered to Jamison. "Remains. Tainted, likely with thallium."

"Jervis, contact Morrow. Tell him we've found the location. Alert the Liaison Division that they can prepare to move in."

They nodded and moved back so the sound of his voice wouldn't carry. They waited long agonising seconds, and then Jervis returned. "Done. He's also sending for Dr Arnett, so she'll be on hand."

Jamison turned. "Take your positions. Watch and listen for the signal."

They moved out, prowling through the underbrush, careful footsteps which sounded like rustling leaves.

Simon's heart thudded slowly. *Soon. Soon you'll be safe, Niamh.*

If only she could hear him.

A shrill cry filled the air, and his muscles tensed. Now was the most dangerous time for Niamh.

Unable to wait, he pulled away from his guards and followed Jamison into the house.

The stink of copper assaulted his nostrils. The deeper in they went, the stronger it became. He didn't notice the wood floors, the vaulted ceilings, or even the lush furnishings.

Bangs and crashes echoed. A scream sounded overhead.

"Here. Down here," Jamison called, and Simon followed the voice, instinct telling him it was towards the door that sealed off the basement.

Simon moved, legs pumping as he crashed past those guarding the barrier and into the dark.

At the bottom, he stilled.

The scene was nightmarish.

A cage in the centre of the room, large and obscuring the view beyond.

He advanced slowly now as he heard the cursing.

His eyes tracked the room. Seeking. Two black membranous things hung from the wall, horrific to view, and he nearly released the contents of his stomach as he realised they were Niamh's wings.

Legs like jelly, he moved closer. There on a table lay a body. She was on her stomach, the skin of her back torn, bones protruding.

These were the remains of her wings.

"Niamh? Oh my gods." He rushed forwards, and though Jamison tried to hold him, he pushed past, resting his hand on her cooling skin.

A faint pulse beat beneath his palm.

"She's... she's still alive," he managed while his gaze took in the ravages, the seeping blood.

The signs of violence on her body, the purple bruising and gashes, sickened him to his very core.

"We need to cover her, my lord."

He nodded mutely as Jamison slid the supplies from his shoulders.

"There's a space blanket inside, but the bleeding is as much a concern as—" The man gulped convulsively as he dragged the cellophane packaging from the metallic blanket and draped it over Niamh. "We need the doctor, quickly."

Without thinking, Simon reached for her face, noting the swelling at her cheek and the dried crusting of vomit at her mouth. "While she's unconscious, take the photos," he instructed Jamison.

He nodded. They'd agreed that if they took Persible alive, they'd need the evidence of what they found.

Jamison worked quickly while Simon kept his vigil beside her.

The sound of a commotion overhead caught his attention. He wanted to go up, to see Persible in chains. The primal instinct to rip apart the one who'd caused his mate so much pain was close to overwhelming, but he somehow managed to control those instincts.

Genevieve would bring in the Liaison Division. They'd extract the information as to the location of Julien Delacorte. She'd already informed him that they had received a dispensation allowing them to use the vampire holding facility to incarcerate and undertake any questioning. Given Julien had been briefly stationed with the female police officer and knew those within the division socially, they'd all agreed the chances of information reaching the man were too high to risk.

While he waited, Simon took out a knife and sliced through the thick ropes tying her to the table.

Her wrists and ankles were torn, oozing messes. Jamison quietly passed him antibacterial wipes to clear the blood. They didn't dress them, though, more than aware that the doctor would need to check for contamination of the wound sites.

So he stayed, terrified she'd wake or the blood loss would steal her away before she could be tended to.

"Show me to her," a female voice imperiously demanded, and he exhaled. The doctor had arrived.

She hurried into the room, her eyes zeroing in on Niamh, now released from the ropes that held her to the tabletop.

"Oh... Oh my. What have they done?"

Simon turned to the shocked woman. "Horrific, isn't it?" The words escaped on a distressed moan.

"Go upstairs. Send for the stretcher team. We need to get her out of here immediately, or otherwise..." She didn't need to say more, just dropped her heavy case and set to work.

Leaving Niamh was a blow to his gut, but he moved up the stairs as the wail of sirens split the early morning air.

Genevieve and a large hulking man emerged from the front vehicle. *David must have stayed behind.* He felt funny, oddly detached, yet he moved to the ambulance where two men waited. "Dr Arnett needs you downstairs. You're going to need the gurney."

They nodded, and he waited, feeling surplus to the requirements right now. He couldn't do anything for Niamh, and he'd only be in the way with Genevieve... and that infuriated him.

He didn't even notice when Morrow stepped up beside him. "Holding up?"

"What?" He almost jumped at the voice, and the odd sense of disembodiment jarred more than before. "Oh, yeah. Just."

The man looked at him oddly. "Bellingham?"

"Huh?"

Morrow grabbed his wrist and dragged him to the car, shoved him into the seat, and pushed a water bottle into his hands. "Drink," he demanded.

"Why?" His voice sounded oddly scratchy.

"Shock. Drink it up, Bellingham, or I'll call a medic over."

Simon upended the bottle and drank deeply despite the churning deep inside.

Morrow grabbed the bottle from his hands. "Breathe. In and out. Take it slow."

The gurney, with Niamh carefully fastened in, exited the house, wheeled by the two medics and Dr Arnett.

Simon rose, and Dr Arnett hurried over to him. "We're taking her to the hospital. She should be okay, but we're going to have to remove part of the humerus bones where her wings extended, Simon. You can follow, but you'd be better off going home first. Showering."

He shook his head. "No. She needs me."

Dr Arnett nodded. "All right, then." She hurried to the back of the ambulance and climbed in. It shot off, sirens and lights breaking the sudden silence.

As it left, Genevieve and Jamison marched a man from the house, his hands cuffed behind him.

Persible.

Without conscious thought, Simon started forwards, brain switching to primal mode.

A hand grasped his shoulder, shoved him back.

Simon roared his displeasure while pack members emerged at a run. "Sit down, or all her pain will count for nothing." The hissed words broke through his enraged haze.

"I..." He shook his head. "Take me to the hospital, Morrow. Please."

The deep and painful grip eased. "Yeah. I'll alert Bailey on the way."

They raced to Morrow's car. Simon dove in the seat, closing the door and donning the belt, while Morrow settled in, starting the engine.

As they drove past the police car, Simon got a good look at Persible.

I'll be seeing you again.

CHAPTER 27

Niamh couldn't say when she understood she was in the hospital. She had vague recollections. Flashes of understanding that made little sense.

Dr Arnett leaning over her. "You'll be all right, Niamh," she'd said. "We're taking you to the hospital. You're safe now."

She wanted to lift her hands, to ask where Simon was, but pain radiated through her body. Her arms were restrained, just like on the table.

She shook wildly, body moving against her will.

"Damn it. Get me that sedative now," Dr Arnett barked.

There was a prick, and then coolness invaded her body, banishing the harsh gnawing heat in every extremity.

"Niamh? Niamh?"

The words echoed and ebbed in her mind before the darkness consumed her.

⁂

"Niamh? Can you hear me?" The touch of a familiar person roused her. Her mind labelled it Finn. But why was Finn here? He was in Ireland, with Danny and the rest of her family.

Her body ached and burned, as if they'd suspended her over a spit, rolling and turning.

A cool cloth slid over her brow. "It's all right, Niamh. I'm here now. Nothing will hurt you again." Simon's rasping tones soothed the uneven beat of her heart.

"Keep talking to her, Simon. It's settling her" came from far away. She knew the voice. Dr Arnett.

Her body felt detached, as if floating, and she welcomed that, because then the pain wafted away.

*S*imon prowled the hallway. Three days had passed since the operation. Dr Arnett had labelled it a success, but that wasn't the concern. At some point, the thallium had contaminated Niamh's system.

Intravenous medication dripped into her veins, slowly and steadily.

The sound of approaching footsteps had him turning. Dr Arnett reached out and touched his hand. "It's early days yet, Simon. We don't quite know how her body will absorb the antibodies we've injected. We need to give it time."

"Her body... She's so small. Fragile."

Dr Arnett patted his hand. "She's not as weak as you think she is. She's fighting back. We're seeing flashes of almost consciousness. She wants to come back. You just have to keep fighting with her."

With a convulsive grip, he seized the doctor's hand. "When? When will she come back?"

Dr Arnett sighed. "I know it's hard for you, but her journey to healing will take a long time. She's lost so much. The innocence that typified her. Her wings." She shrugged. "Let's focus on what we can be grateful for, though, shall we? She's alive and I believe will make a full recovery."

The heavy weight of pain and anguish in his heart lightened. "You're sure?"

"I am, Simon." The doctor blinked. "It won't happen overnight, but she will improve. Be prepared though, it's going to take time. Just how long I don't know."

Simon nodded and hoped the doctor was correct. That Niamh would make a full recovery. Anything else was unacceptable. He sucked in a deeply unsteady breath and looked to the ceiling, willing away the burn in his eyes. The alternative, a bleak possibility still, was just too shattering to consider.

Niamh opened her eyes. The room was unfamiliar, though it held the smell of cleansers she associated with Dr Arnett's office.

Her body felt... frail. There was no strength in her arms. Lifting a finger left her gasping, and her eyes wanted to droop. The *beep beep* of a machine sounded beside her.

Her back ached, and she moved to shift.

"Stay still, Niamh."

Simon came into view. He looked ragged, as if he'd been through a battle lasting weeks. His eyes were rimmed with dark shadows, hair roughened his jawline, and his face was thinner. Drawn.

"Simon?"

He nodded, Adam's apple bobbing as he swallowed thickly. "Do you know—" His voice cracked. She watched him lick his lips. "Do you know where you are?"

"The hospital, I think. But my wings... Someone will see."

His gaze darkened, and he glanced away. When he turned back, pain had overtaken his face. "They're gone, Niamh. Do you remember that?"

"What's gone?" Panic settled in her chest, ballooning within her. "What's gone?"

Simon's hand settled against her cheek. "He... Persible took them from you."

"No... No, no, no!" She made to rise, but the effort had her guts churning. The *beep beep* sped up. "My wings!"

"I'm sorry, Niamh. We were too late."

Hot tears scalded her face. "Why?"

Simon's face darkened. "He's mad. Certifiable, but Cressida, Genevieve, and the Liaison Division are gathering as much information as possible, Niamh. He'll pay. I'll make sure of it."

The intense emotions drained her. Exhausted, she let her eyes flutter shut and gave in to sleep.

*S*imon slumped into the chair beside her bed. A week to open her eyes, and he'd ruined it by telling her about her wings. He dropped his head to the sheets as the curtain slid open.

"Did she wake?"

Dr Arnett shuffled in, and he raised his head. "Briefly."

"What happened?"

"She knows about her wings." His answer was brief. Curt.

Dr Arnett's face tightened. "I see. How did she react?"

"Badly."

He watched as she stalked to the heart monitor, checked the readout. "Panic, yes. To be expected."

Simon hated the clinical fashion she used to consider Niamh. Impersonal, even. "Now that she's regained consciousness, how soon can she come home?"

At least at home, she'd be able to rest without the poking and prodding of the medicals. She could take her time and heal. Emotionally and physically.

"That depends on Niamh. I need to assess her mental state before we decide."

He must have telegraphed his discontent with her words, because before he could speak, she held her hand up. "Listen. The trauma of losing a limb is difficult for most to bear, but she's a fairy. The wings aren't just part of her body, they also affect her ability to be what she is." Dr Arnett shook her head. "I know a little of the procreation functions. The wings allow her to perform what is necessary, right? Now, I've actually sought help from the elder fairy. I know there's more at play here, that there's a prophecy, but what we don't know is how this will affect Niamh inside her mind. Her view of herself. She's a strong woman, but this drives to the very heart of her understanding of self. She needs time and may need therapy. Because none of us have really ever dealt with this kind of situation, we just don't know. That's why I can't say when, Simon."

He huffed out a breath. "I... I understand."

"Maybe not yet, but you're trying. That will mean a lot, but you must take your lead from her. Now go home. Shower. Eat. Rest."

Once more he made to argue, and she held up her hand. "That's an order, or I will contact the Council and they can strong-arm you."

She meant it. There was a stinging sincerity to her words, so he gave a deep nod. "Niamh?"

"If she wakes while you're gone, I'll be there. It's why you're paying me to be her personal physician, isn't it?"

That was true. He also knew she'd found a locum to step into her practice until they released Niamh from the hospital. He didn't care what it cost him, just so long as Niamh had the care and attention she deserved.

*N*iamh woke. The pain in her back was still there, though much less. With care, she turned her head, noting Dr Arnett's presence.

"What... what are you doing here?" she croaked.

"I'm standing in for Simon. I sent him home to rest. He's been here twenty-three out of ever twenty-four hours of each day."

"How long have I been here?"

The woman smiled. "Just shy of a week, my dear." Her smile melted. "How do you feel?"

"Awful," Niamh answered. "My back hurts, and Simon said my

wings…" She couldn't finish the words, too horrified by the reality to say it aloud.

"Do you want to know about your back?"

Niamh considered the question. "I… Yes." Her eyes pricked with tears. "What did he do to me?"

The doctor scooted the seat closer, the scrape louder than the sudden rapid beat of her heart.

"Persible abducted you. Held you for two days. Simon rallied his team, but even with the best trackers and the help of the vampires, it took time to work out where you were. When Simon found you, Persible had already removed your wings."

Greasy waves of horror spread through Niamh. "What… what else?"

"When Simon's team found you, you were spreadeagle on a mortuary table. You'd been badly beaten, Niamh. He exposed the ends of the humerus bones, and you were bleeding. A lot. In order to save your life, we had to excise the bone ends, find the source of the bleeding, and, well…" Dr Arnett shrugged. "We also found you'd absorbed thallium through your skin, and it poisoned your system. That accounts for the delirium and weakness. And hair loss."

Niamh wanted to raise her arms to see what had become of her appearance, but the weight was too great. "My hair is gone?"

Dr Arnett shook her head. "Not all of it, my dear, just clumps. We've been treating you intravenously with a range of supplements, doses of Prussian blue in saline pushes, and antibiotics."

"I'll never fly again." The words slipped out before she could stop them.

"No, my dear." She touched Niamh's hand, grounding her.

The future appeared so bleak. Niamh wanted to curse and scream, but all she could do was lie there and feel numb.

Surely this would put paid to any hopes she might have harboured with the man she loved. What was best? How to react? "When he comes back, I…" She almost gagged on what she needed to say. "I don't want to see him. Send him away."

She stared straight ahead, refusing to look at the woman beside her. She had to be strong and let him go.

"No, Niamh. I won't tell him that."

"Why?" she cried and turned, feeling the tug of healing skin. "Why won't you tell him? With me, he has no future. No children. No—"

"I spoke with the elder fairy, Niamh. There's a prophecy. One of genuine love. One of walking it together. To finish it, the optimal word is together. Not one or the other. She also said there is another, of the melding of paranormals. I've spoken with Samra, from one of the vampire houses. She found a record of another kind. One that points to the melding of two kinds of others. In order for that to happen, there must be sacrifice."

Niamh screwed up her face. "I don't understand."

Dr Arnett leaned in. "You've already sacrificed your wings, Niamh. It doesn't mean you have to sacrifice love. I wonder if you two, together, will be the sealing of connection between were and fairy. The two of you, bringing them ever closer."

Niamh blinked, confused. "What do you mean?"

"It was always going to be difficult with you as a fairy and him as a were. Interspecies breeding isn't something we understand well. All we know is that one tiny strand of DNA is the basis of all paranormal beings."

She nodded, understanding the basics of their genetic makeup.

"I have always posited that we can breed across species. We know Genevieve is one such hybrid. But you and Simon, maybe that will be another. The melding of two strong genetic strands creating something more."

Niamh stared at her. "We could...?"

Dr Arnett grinned. "If Genevieve's parents could, then so could you. You wouldn't be giving up anything, Niamh. Isn't it worth taking the chance?"

CHAPTER 28

Simon eased Niamh from the car. "Let me carry you in," he urged, but she shook her head, moving gingerly.

"I can walk."

He knew she found the careful touches annoying, but his psyche demanded that he treat her like spun glass, fragile.

"Okay," he agreed but stayed close by. Bailey or Ulrich could bring in her bag and the floral tributes and plants many had gifted her during her hospitalisation.

Inside, she eased herself down into a plush seat in the lounge. Simon was thankful he'd cleared everyone from the house as he crouched down beside her. "Do you want a drink or...?"

"A glass of water would be welcome."

He noted the fine beading of sweat at her upper lip. Much as he wanted to wipe it away, he was firmly reminded of the therapist's words.

"She's got to find her own way. Mollycoddling will set her back or impede her healing. If she asks, then great. But also weigh that up with the awareness that you mustn't enable her to become a cripple either. It's a fine line."

"But how do I know?" Simon asked.

The therapist shook his head. "You'll only be aware of whether you've done it right later on. None of this is an exact science. She's got to deal with the trauma, and I'd recommend she enter therapy in due course. But she must learn to come to terms with what's happened, find a healthy way to accept it and move on. Create a new self-awareness."

Three days after that discussion, he remained as confused as he'd been immediately afterwards.

He rose and headed for the kitchen, grabbed a glass, and filled it with water, taking a moment to balance his emotions. The therapist had pointed out that he was going to be playing a major role in her recovery. Or at least he would be if that was what Niamh decided she wanted. So far it appeared to be the case.

Once he'd returned to the lounge, he handed her the glass, watching as she drank deeply.

She set the glass down and wiped her mouth. "We need to talk, Simon. Dr Arnett paid me a visit in the hospital." With halting words, she relayed what she'd been told, the deductions they'd drawn. "So I guess the first question, and the most important, is whether you're repulsed by the loss of my wings."

She couldn't have shocked him further. "I didn't just love you for your wings, Niamh. They were beautiful, part of you, but you're so much more than simply the fairy I first met. You're the woman who completes me. I love you. You know that already. I want to take you to mate, but I would say nothing until you asked. The therapist—"

Niamh's laugh was tense. "He told me it was my decision. That I was the centre, but I told him, the same as I'm telling you know, it's us. That's the key. I love you, Simon, but it's going to take time. I have to come to terms with both what I lost and what I stand to gain."

He moved to embrace her, but she stopped him. "Wait. You need to know it's going to take time. The scars... Dr Arnett showed them to me. They're... they're horrible, but they're part of who I am now. The person I have to make myself into. The person I have to come to know. For the next little while, I would like to move back into the spare room."

He had to hold on to his emotions at her bold announcement.

As if she understood, she ducked her head. "This isn't about you, Simon. It's about me. Please." When she glanced up, there were tears glinting in her eyes.

"If that's what you need," he ground out. "You tell me what you need, and if I can, I'll give it to you, Niamh."

She nodded. "I know. That's part of why I need to do this. I know it's hurting you, Simon. I'm sorry, and if it's too much, I'll go stay with Finn and Danny."

Now he rose, stalked over, and knelt before her, his hand shaking as he cupped her jaw. "Don't leave me, Niamh."

Her eyes closed on a sob. "I don't want to. I just... I need to find my balance."

Niamh healed over the next weeks. She took the time to meet Frederick and Marta, to cuddle the baby, and watch the youngsters roll and play.

She spent time with Finn and Danny, who mourned the loss of her wings. Her banishment wasn't overturned, but Esmerelda granted a dispensation allowing her to speak with her parents on the phone. Her parents were concerned but had settled, the witch informed her, once aware they must be patient and that she would heal, eventually.

Simon watched her, cared for her, but didn't baby her either.

Today was her first day back at the clinic. Her hands shook as she inserted the key into the lock and let herself in, Bailey and Ulrich shadowing her. It was the one thing Simon insisted on, and she'd not yet grown accustomed to walking alone anywhere. It was the one crutch she allowed herself.

She keyed in her password after booting the computer system.

The day's appointments flicked onto the screen, and she bit her lip, finding an email from Lisa.

Welcome back, Niamh.

I'm available on call for the next week or two. Dr Arnett insisted that you should have a fallback in case it all became too much, so I've a temp trained to fill in should you need time. Her details are in the black book in the top drawer.

The patient files were last updated on Friday night.

I know all the patients you've had contact with will be pleased to see you return.

Above all, though, remember that you're not just capable but an integral part of our community.

We've missed you.

Lisa

The words made her want to cry. Everyone had been kind, but now she felt the urgency to prove herself. Not just to others but also to herself.

"Come on. You're not a wimp, Niamh. Now, what's the first thing to do?"

She glanced at the patient list and the symptoms or known ongoing ailments. She set up the treatment room and, finally satisfied, settled once more in her seat. The day was going to be long and tiring, but she was more than ready for the challenge.

Dr Arnett entered the building, her gaze falling on Niamh. "How do you feel today? Ready to return to work?"

Niamh smiled. "Yes. I've missed this."

Dr Arnett enfolded her in a hug, something Niamh was rapidly becoming used to from the doctor. "Good. Now if it's too much, Lisa has—"

"I read her email, but I'll call her in if necessary. The treatment room is ready, and I'll open the door in ten minutes. I'm going to make a tea and settle myself first. Then I'll check the phones to see if there's any urgent calls. I see Lisa has allocated three urgent booking spots today."

Dr Arnett smiled warmly. "Fine, then. Get that tea, and we'll get started."

Simon kept his cell beside him all day, Bailey or Ulrich feeding him updates as the hours passed.

Dr Arnett had been insistent that if Niamh looked fatigued, she'd send her home.

Meanwhile, he dealt with the business at hand.

Jessica settled in the seat opposite him, her eyes alight with mischief. "So you set her free, did you?"

"She needs to re-enter the world. So long as Bailey and Ulrich are there, she should be fine." He glanced through the papers, signed the indicated spots. "Any more trouble with the Council members?"

Jessica shook her head. "Not since the incident." That was the term she used to describe his absence during the long days of Niamh's abduction and subsequent hospitalisation.

"Good. And the Persible trial?" He struggled to hold on to his emotions.

"Simon, do you really want me to stand in for you?"

As always, he took a moment, centred himself before answering. "Yes. She's my mate, Jessica. You know controlling it in this situation is precarious. If we're going to petition for judicial rights, we must prove that we can be objective even under the most extenuating circumstances." Gods, how he hated the political smarminess and correct language he had to spin. If he had his way, he'd have torn the man limb from limb. As it was, the trial would take every ounce of willpower to handle in a humane—though not human, for he'd never been one—fashion.

"All right, well, they set the initial trial for June 21 next year. It's the earliest date they can grant us. Meantime, the Senate will accept our petition, and I've already got a team on it. We're drawing in the vampires too. They're willing to support our petition, but in return, they'd like a formalised Memorandum of Understanding."

"All right, what would that entail?"

"I'm not sure, but Cressida, Xavier, and Daniel would like an appointment to set up an initial scoping committee. I would support it, Simon." The earnestness that she radiated matched his agreement.

"Okay. We need to take this to the Council as a priority. Add it to the agenda for next week's meeting, and let Cressida's people know."

"Oh, one more thing." Jessica bit her lip and extended an envelope. "Niamh gave me this. Said to give it to you in the early afternoon."

He frowned, then took the missive and nodded.

Jessica left the room, and he broke the seal.

Simon,

First, I have to thank you for giving me time and space. I know it's been hard.

I have decided.

If you're willing, I'd like to discuss it with you tonight.

If you could arrange a meal, I'll arrange the dessert.

Niamh

His hands shook.

What had she decided? The only thing he could take any surety from was the comment about the dessert. Just like the first night they were together.

The doorbell rang, and he rose as Jessica called, "Can you get that?"

He turned the knob, and there stood Amalia. "These are for you." She thrust a bunch of flowers into his hands. Buttercups, marigolds, and primroses.

His heart thudded in his chest. "I..."

"Also the dessert platter and some wine. Celebrating tonight, are we?"

"Uh..." The words he should answer with strangled him.

She smiled. "It's okay. There's also a note." She slid it on top of the box.

He stepped back and closed the door once she left, then took the items to the kitchen, emotion welling within him.

He leaned against the countertop and opened the envelope.

Simon,
Roses are red
Violets are blue
My man is still the best
Because I love you.
Niamh XXX

Tears burned in his eyes, and he dashed them away, his heart expanding in his chest.

*N*iamh turned the key in the lock, letting herself in.

The small bag she'd tucked away in her underwear drawer was an emotion magnet. Over the last few days, she'd planned tonight down to the last detail.

"Just so long as it goes to plan," she whispered.

He'd been so patient, waiting for her to decide where she stood and if she was ready for this.

She'd been religious in attending her therapy sessions and knew he'd also gone to several. Physically, she was in excellent condition, and the time she'd spent with the elder fairy had also aided her mental recovery. It was rare that a fairy lost their wings, though it happened, and she'd contacted a few.

Returning to work had also soothed her. Today, she'd even received her enrolment package from the healer's guild and would begin her studies after the Christmas season.

The only aspect of her life not yet assured was the situation between her and Simon.

She knew he was ready and willing, but as her therapist had pointed out, wanting differed greatly from happening.

Simon called from the kitchen, and she ducked her head in, pleased to see her deliveries had arrived.

"Welcome home," he whispered against her lips.

She leaned in, accepting the soft caress, and smiled.

"I'm going to shower and change. How long till dinner?"

"How soon do you want to eat?"

Glancing out the window, she noted the darkness had settled in the short while since she'd parked and entered the house. "How about when I come down? Say fifteen minutes?"

He nodded, and she left him there, scurrying up the staircase.

Once in the bedroom, she stripped off her clothes and headed for the attached bathroom. She hoped this might be the last time she used it. Nights were long without Simon there embracing her.

The water sluiced over her body, and she hurried through washing and then shaving her legs before stepping out and towelling her hair dry. It hadn't fully regrown yet, but she'd found a ponytail or loose bun hid most of the damage.

Padding to the bedroom, she reached into the top dresser drawer and pulled out the underwear she'd chosen, the filmy lace little more than tiny scraps of material. The cups barely covered the swells of her breasts, and the panties gently abraded the swollen mound of her nether region.

With shaking fingers, she applied a light layer of makeup, then reached into the cupboard for the dress she'd bought. It slid over her body, cupping curves, giving nothing away of what lay underneath.

Heading down to the kitchen, she found him waiting, his suit pants and immaculate white shirt hiding the body she missed so much. He leaned in and kissed her. "You look amazing."

She grinned and followed him to the table set for two. The flowers she'd sent—and she'd almost cancelled the order until Amalia told her it was an amazing thing to do for her man—sat slightly to the left of centre.

The meal was concealed beneath warming domes until he tugged the covers up and away.

Her eyes dropped to the food, and she smiled. "You remembered."

"I had some help, though. Unlike you, cordon bleu is a little beyond my cooking skill."

He offered her wine, and she nodded.

During the main course, she told him a little about her day. When they finished, she offered to help clear the table, but he refused her assistance. "Wait in the lounge. I'll bring the dessert through. The fire is already lit."

She settled on the long seat, hoping he'd take the hint, and when he slid down beside her, Niamh sighed and moved a little closer.

"I wanted to talk with you. About us. I've had time to think." She turned to look at him, hoping he'd understood the notes and gifts. "I've missed you, Simon. Every day and every night, there's an emptiness, and I want the closeness we had. I miss being in your arms and your loving."

His smile turned lopsided. "Oh gods, Niamh. I've missed you too. I've given you your space and tried to understand." His hand gripped hers, shaking with emotion.

"I know. That's what's made this easier. I love you, Simon. For a while I didn't want to. I tried to turn away, but Dr Arnett told me not to. I spoke with other fairies and asked them about... you know."

He nodded. "I guessed as much. But, Niamh, I don't care about others. I want to be with you. To share my life with you. To marry you."

"I know. It's what I want too."

He reached into his pocket. "I've been carrying this the whole time you've been healing. Three months," he sputtered, "burning through my pocket."

He tugged out a jewellery case, slid it open so she could see a stunning emerald surrounded with diamonds. "Marry me, Niamh."

"I want to say yes, but I need to tell you, I may or may not conceive—"

"I don't care. Marry me."

She gripped both his cheeks. "Listen, because my answer depends on yours. Do you understand what I just said?"

He nodded. "I do. But, Niamh, that's what I'm saying. Children or no, I love you. Marry me."

"Yes," she whispered.

He released a shuddering breath, took the ring, and reverently slid it onto her finger.

"Will you also mate with me?"

"Yes."

He tugged her up and into his arms. "Do you want dessert now?"

She shook her head. "No, I just want you."

EPILOGUE

Niamh looked at the tiny packet.

"Are you going to open it?" Simon's voice came over her shoulder, and she looked up.

"You knew I bought it?"

He shrugged. "A hunch."

"What if it's negative?"

"Then it is," he answered. "Go. Take the test."

Niamh bit her lip. "I want to, but I'm scared, Simon."

He cupped her cheeks with both hands. "So am I, Niamh. But there won't be an answer until you get in there. I'll be here waiting, whatever the result."

Niamh retreated to the bathroom and used the test. After washing her hands, she brought the test back out to join him once more.

"How long?" Simon asked his mate.

"Five minutes," she replied, her eyes having taken on a golden tinge since the night of their engagement when they'd finally completed the ritual.

His body ached with the memory.

"Niamh?" he'd called, his body tight and hers already damp and ready for the carnal invasion.

"Please, Simon. Fill me."

He'd slid deep within her, slowly making them one. His fangs descended. "I want... Niamh, mate with me?"

"Yes," she answered, her eyes glowing in the half light of the fire. There in the lounge, he'd slid his teeth into her shoulder. She'd arched and cried out, and then he'd felt the twin sting as she returned the favour.

He'd felt the magic and knew she did too, their bodies moving, entwined.

"Simon?"

Her words jerked him back. "Yeah?"

"Has it been long enough?" She took his hand in hers, shaking, and he tugged her into his embrace, cursing himself. He checked the clock, made the calculations. "Yeah."

She picked up the test from where she'd set it, scanning.

One positive... two.

"Oh gods."

"What?" Did it mean what he hoped?

"I'm pregnant, Simon. We're expecting a baby!"

He kissed her then, satisfaction suffusing him because he had Niamh and now this precious bundle to look forward to.

"I love you, Niamh."

"And I love you," she told him.

Did you enjoy this book by Imogene Nix?
There's more on the following pages. Just keep turning to see what else.

Genevieve is many things, but no single title fits her quite as accurately as '*mutt*'—the one bestowed by her vicious ex-boyfriend. She's built a life, far from the family who've disowned her—one she's proud of—as a police officer with the Paranormal Liaison Division, and hiding from the world.

David is brittle from his experiences with his ex-wife Alexa, the truth his parents duped him his whole life, and he's trying to come to terms with the fallout of those beliefs, running a nest and feeling like an imposter.

A chance meeting between Genevieve and David opens up an opportunity for hope amid the grim realities of paranormal warfare.

Trusting each other may be their only choice, but the past always bites back and this time is no different.

"Do you know anything about...?" David waved his arm, and Daniel shook his head.

David clamped his arm on his shoulder and squeezed. He knew he was pale, but the reality of the situation impinged.

Hope had glanced at him, smiled tremulously, but didn't approach.

"Are you okay?" Daniel's question swam through David's brain.

He cleared his throat, considered the man before him. "I don't... I'm resigning my commission and plan to seek a place in a new house." The words erupted from him, but once out, David relaxed.

Daniel frowned. "Today?"

He shook his head. "No. When the mess with Attar is done. I've hung in only because... It was Hope who kept me together once I came to terms with what had been done. I treated her badly and so did my parents, and I feel dirty because I believed everything I was told. Now it's hard to stay after..." David shrugged.

"But if Hope forgives you, surely the situation can be resolved?"

"No, Daniel. Everyone knows what I did. What *we* did. How we took her—Alexa's—side and left Hope to suffer the consequences of the lies. It just... it doesn't feel right, you know? She's built something good and true. I can't muddy it any longer than necessary. She needs to rebuild her life free of that taint."

Daniel frowned. "If you need to move, you would be more than welcome with me. I can talk to Javed..."

"No. But thank you." David shook his head. "When it's done... Once Attar is defeated, I'm thinking of going somewhere else."

Sucking in a deep breath, he stepped back around Daniel and wandered to the other side of the room.

Several Months Later

David looked down at his hands. Instead of the neatly manicured nails he'd always sported, ragged edges betrayed the rage he'd held at bay over the last several months.

Now this. The parchment paper in his grip crackled, and he released the hold slightly, forcing himself to read the front page.

Referring to the decree made in this cause... the marriage between the aforementioned Plaintiff and Defendant be dissolved unless sufficient cause be shown to the court...

He wasn't unhappy with the outcome. Neither was he ecstatic. It wasn't the way he'd planned for his life to proceed.

Alexa had lied to him. Made a dupe of him. There'd been no child, and she'd blinded him to truths he should have noted. The betrayal ran deep. She'd colluded with his father, alienated his mother, and damaged the relationship he had with his sister.

The situation felt untenable, really.

But still... The life he'd planned to make was over. Deleted with the stroke of a pen by a Family Court judge.

Slumping back into his chair, David surveyed the room. It was new, pale-coloured walls in a strange boxlike building, yet there was a charm to it. The kind he hadn't ever felt in the old-world manor where he'd grown to adulthood.

He sighed.

Dawn had passed some three hours before, and while he, along with his master, Javed, had agreed the house didn't require an external office set-up at this point, it felt odd to be ordering a coffee and still wearing the lounging pants he'd tugged on after showering at nine in the morning.

The phone buzzed and broke the internal ruminations that occupied his mind.

He answered with a curt "David."

"Sir, we have an officer of the law here. They say it's important they speak with you. Something to do with a situation with the vampires."

"Fine. Give me a moment, then send him in."

"Her, sir."

He blinked. "Of course."

Letting go of the button, he rose from his chair, straightened his clothing—the teachings of his mother still held tight—before lowering himself into the chair, preparing for whatever came to pass.

The door opened, and a slim, dark-haired woman entered the room. She wasn't tall, and her features were regular. Her hair, tied into a neat and tidy braid, was dark brown, though her eyes were a golden green colour.

The impressive creases, carefully aligned in her uniform, and the shine of her shoes told him she was either a new officer or one of those committed to her job. He had a feeling it was the second option.

"David Jardin?"

He inclined his head, and the woman stood, facing him.

Discomfort flowed. In his world, you asked women to sit; they were coddled and kept at home until they married. This woman might look soft, but he noted a spark of something in her eyes and the ramrod straightness of her spine. This was no meek and biddable woman here. It was perverse, but he didn't offer the seat.

"You wanted to talk to me about the vampire attacks?"

She blinked. "Uh, yes. I wanted to make some further enquiries. My name's Officer Fernly, from the Liaison Division, and I need to check some facts to determine—"

His brow furrowed as he concentrated on what had taken place the evening before. He'd found a briefing paper on his desk when he'd entered that morning.

"Oh yes," he interrupted. Something about this woman put him on guard.

She flipped open the tiny notepad she carried. "We have reports of a man attacked by what he believes was a vampire. He escaped, but it terrified him. He's lost a lot of blood and may very well require assistance coming to terms with the attack."

"And what do you want me to do for you today, Officer Fernly?"

"It's been suggested that it's more than just a single attack. We haven't been informed of such a circumstance, and if there's a likelihood of danger to the public—"

He raised a hand. "I'm limited on what I can divulge, Officer." Now he indicated to a seat and watched as she slowly lowered herself to the padded cushion. The closing of her eyes and the gentle exhalation betrayed her emotional state.

"You were on duty last night and attended this call. Yet you're on duty this morning."

The woman seated opposite him glanced in his direction. "I work the hours necessary to get the job done."

Available from Love Books Publishing
books2read.com/ImmortalConsequences

Direct Autographed Copy
https://www.imogenenix.net/AsDawnBreaks

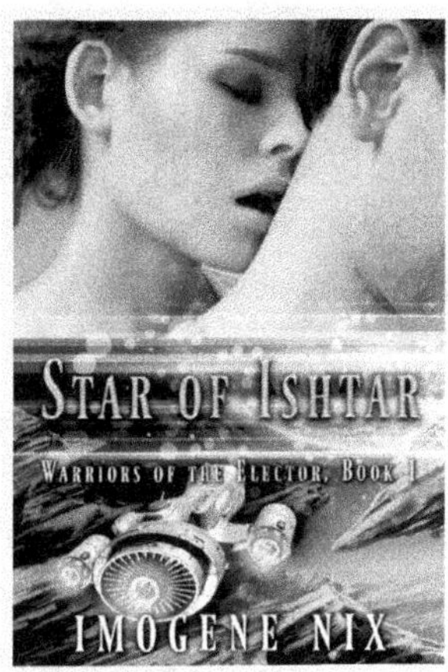

Warriors of the Elector
Book One

The first time Elara laid eyes on Grayson was when he rescued her from the clutches of a madman and his scientists who were kidnapping humans and conducting horrific experiments on them. That was years ago. In spite of her attempts to deepen their relationship, they remained nothing more than close friends.Now Elara is a medic with the Admiralty, and she knows what she wants. It's been Grayson since the beginning. When Elara is stationed on the *Star of Ishtar*, she arrives with a plan to further her career. But this time her plan has an added bonus—to finally get her man.

Grayson's spent years fighting the connection between himself and Elara. He's certain it only exist because he saved her life. But his will is failing, and he fears he just might give in to temptation.

"I finally made it." Elara Sudonne watched as the hull of the *Star of Ishtar* loomed in the inky darkness. She clutched her hands tightly together as the shuttle approached the hulking battleship.

This would be her new home and first combat ST placement for the Earth Empire. She quaked inwardly with nerves but fought to keep her serene exterior. Previously her deployments had consisted solely of on-planet expeditions and in rehabilitation and dirtside facilities. When the chance had arisen to move to the battleship, she'd grabbed it with both hands.

The frigid air chilled her bones as she sat in her shuttle seat, but a trickle of sweat inched its way down her back under the fresh gray wool flight uniform. Little puffs of vapor escaped her mouth as she rubbed her arms. Nerves stretched tight, she looked through the small portal at the front of the vessel. She wanted to tug at the collar that somehow seemed to have grown tighter as the ship loomed ahead, but instead she firmed her mouth, straightened her spine, and concentrated on the future.

"So damned long." She'd been working toward this outcome since the day Grayson Myatt and Duvall McCord had saved her from her Ru'Edan captors. She was lucky, she'd survived the 'experimentation' of the Ru'Edan leader Crick Sur Banden's scientists. "And all I have to remind me are my scars." She didn't grin at her own joke.

The person seated behind her jostled but she ignored it, lost in her memories. On that day, so very long ago, the young Elara, fresh-faced and with idealistic views of the empire, was taken from the mall where she'd been shopping with friends, thrust into the back of a transport vehicle, and given to the Ru'Edan scientists to experiment on.

For days they'd worked on her and others, seeking an average pain threshold of humans, slicing her skin then noting reactions and how long it took to heal. They'd cut her arms, body, and even her face, and now she carried the extensive scarring of the exercise as a reminder to herself and others of what they were fighting for. Freedom. The freedom of Earth and its allied planets.

She'd never relinquished hope, it had been her constant companion as she fought against the all-consuming terror. Then they'd found her in that dirty, disused warehouse. They'd found others too, in various states of death and decay. The smells of despair had filled the air with a fetid ripeness that she'd never been able to forget.

Since that day she'd promised herself that she would pay the Ru'Edan back for what they'd done to her. What they'd taken from her. Over the years, she tempered and honed the rage while remaining adamant that she would see the final act played out. She couldn't physically fight, but she had learned about trauma, knew it and understood how it affected a person, and used it as a weapon.

The iron will forged through her experiences had fed her determination, and she'd applied herself to study, finishing in the top ten percent of her class. She entered the medical program at the academy, working hard to excel. Her family remained supportive if perplexed as to why she had chosen to keep reminding herself of what had happened.

The maw of the *Star of Ishtar* loomed closer, opening its cavernous mouth as she watched through the portal. She could hear the voices of the shuttle crew signaling their intention to enter and land, the tinny confirmation coming swiftly. She watched avidly while the shuttle manoeuvered, imagining the invisible shields dropping to allow it entry.

Her hands twisted with fear and anger, but she tamped down her emotions. Anger never helped anyone. Staying strong, knowing your history, and ensuring it couldn't be repeated, they were the answers, she told herself firmly, pulling herself from the grip of a dark past so horrific she still saw it in her dreams. She pushed it away to the recesses of her mind and focused on what she was about to do.

A squark overhead, the usual mechanical sound that alerted all on board to a transmission by the captain, caught her attention. "Attention all passengers. We are entering the shuttle bay. Please ensure when you disembark you remove all personal items. Move beyond the white line and wait for your designation."

The lights of the bay flashed as they entered, and once again Elara marveled at how far humanity had moved since they had first walked the Earth. She saw the opening of the structure as the shuttle moved into the bay, inching forward slowly until it stopped its ponderous motion and began its descent to the floor. Something deep inside warmed even as the shuttle's environmental systems began to synchronise with the cooler temperature of the *Star of Ishtar*, and she felt a smile crawl its way over her face.

Elara breathed in deeply, inhaling the metallic-tasting, recycled air and welcoming the calmness that settled on her body. Her eyes closed as she filled her lungs. "I'm here." There was more than a little satisfaction in her tone, and she smiled. She slowly exhaled, finding that centre of peace she relied on.

A loud thud and clank echoed as the deep drone split the air. The engines were powering down, and there she was, on one of the Earth Empire's Emeritus class battleships. She sat in her seat, waiting for the all clear from the captain, and once it sounded through the cabin, she rose, tugging at the webbing belt and disengaging it.

The small backpack beside her was all she carried as she made her way to the exit, not needing to duck as so many others did. She stepped through the door, her hands gripping the rail of the cold, metal stairs which connected to the side of the grey shuttle.

She clambered down them slowly, savoring the experience. The sting of the cold on her hands from the stairs, frigid from even their brief exposure to the blackness of space, made her flinch inwardly. The shuttle journey from the Admiralty's strategic base at Aenna to their current position had taken just over an hour, but the whole time it felt like her heart had been in her throat. Her mouth was dry as she followed the new recruits from the ship into the landing bay. She stopped, silently noting the slight mustiness of the air, the recycled quality easily recognizable. Everything, including the oxygen, needed recycling in space.

All around her people swarmed, either around the ships or into the dogleg line that now formed ahead of her. Someone had opened the baggage locker of the shuttle, and the sound of dropping bags hitting the plascrete floor echoed in the air. Another crewmember guided trolleys to the other side of the shuttle, pulling out boxes with important day-to-day items for the ship, including vaccines and plants. She watched briefly, all the while listening to the alien cacophony. Voices called in welcome to old crewmembers, while new ones watched, many goggle-eyed in the fresh uniforms of newly minted officers and crewmembers.

Her gaze flicked around quickly, taking in the sights, sounds, and smells, pungent with oils and grease; burning smells from the scorched plascrete and the press of sweaty or nervous bodies. She joined the line silently, tacking onto the end, and stayed at parade rest, knowing the welcoming voice would cut through the air soon enough. She felt somehow disconnected from the main throng. Perhaps the knowledge that this was the outcome she had worked for years to achieve set her apart. However, still, she felt so...distant from everything around her. She smiled secretly at the bout of whimsy.

"Attention!" The voice boomed out over the plascrete of the docking bay, and she snapped her body into position, noting the commander who had bellowed the words. Technically, she outranked most members aboard the *Star of Ishtar*, except for the command and leadership staff, but she knew all newcomers had to join the welcoming parade, regardless of rank.

Fleet Captain Elphin came into view, his tired features topped by salt-and-pepper grey hair, which highlighted his cool blue eyes. Elara also recognised a body prone to a little middle-aged thickness. Following behind him was his second-in-command, Duvall McCord. A young up-and-coming officer, his status as a fast-tracking officer heading toward his own command, with Elphin both his mentor and captain, had become almost legendary at the academy.

She looked closely at McCord, noting the dynamic drive of his actions and movements. Soon he would achieve a promotion to captain, and she rejoiced for her friend. She'd followed his career with interest and had to tamp down a smile as his eyes betrayed the shock of seeing her before settling into their flat command persona. So he hadn't been apprised of her deployment, she noted, and she had to restrain the tiny feeling of surprise and satisfaction. She filed that snippet of information away.

She caught sight of the man standing behind Duvall. Grayson Myatt. He'd made her heart beat faster for years. Tall and blond with a muscular build and a sexy, tight, little butt, he had pools of deep-blue eyes that had always made her think of forever. He had a growth of stubble on his chiseled jaw, and her fingers itched to touch his perfect lips. Yes, since the day he'd found her in that nasty warehouse tied down like a ragged animal, she'd worshipped him from afar.

Now she had her opportunity to tangle with him, hopefully much closer than any chance that had ever come her way before. With a sigh, she pulled her gaze back to the captain and forced herself to concentrate on his words. She couldn't afford to have her commanding officer angry due to her being distracted.

"Welcome to the *Star of Ishtar*. Most academy recruits want to join us because of what we represent, but on this ship, we only take the best of the best. So, if you made it here, you're the ones we wanted to take a look at. Getting here is only the first step. Staying here is harder to achieve. Our people are the best. Earn your place, and in return, we'll make you one of our crew—a member of the *Star of Ishtar*. Only the best and the brightest wear our uniform and badge. You'll be expected to perform to your absolute limit then give some more. We don't tolerate people who don't pull their weight. Do us proud and wear your uniform with pride." The captain looked out over the new members of his crew. His voice had echoed during his speech, and now it died away.

He scanned the faces before him, and she could almost read his thoughts. There were new security officers and a smattering of other crew. Some of them were young and impressionable, and she knew a few wouldn't make the cut as crewmembers. Others would carve out their place on the *Star of Ishtar* and move to better positions and placements, like she would: the new SurgiTech, a younger female, experienced but untried on board a ship. She smiled at that thought.

Some of those who stood with her would be replaced as they failed the exacting standards the captain set. She'd heard that he was a firm captain, fair but demanding. He'd have to be to command this ship. The Ishtar had well over five hundred at full capacity, and the captain could select their placements as his command staff saw fit from the many who applied to join the crew. She sensed his satisfaction with the choices in the relaxation of his body.

Abruptly, he turned to Duvall, breaking her study of him. "Get them to where they need to present themselves." His words echoed as he walked away. He had a purposeful stride. Quick but unhurried, like he knew where he was going and how to get there. A man who knew how to get what he wanted. Someone to respect and admire.

"My name is Commander Duvall McCord. I am your second-in-command, and my direct subordinate is Commander Grayson Myatt. While you are aboard the *Star of Ishtar* you will be required to fulfill your duties efficiently. As Captain Elphin said, do your job right and you will be one of ours, with all the benefits that come with being a crewmember of the *Star of Ishtar*."

He paused and eyeballed each of the newer recruits, those fresh from the academy. Many of them paled under his gaze, and she smiled inwardly. Even the older people in the line seemed to quake beneath his scowl. He'd always had that air of innate authority, even when barely out of the academy himself. She knew his methods and watched him make full use of the carefully practiced tone of presence.

"Each of you has been assigned. You will present yourselves to the chief of your section. Those details will be found in your orders. Commander Myatt has organised a team to escort you to your cabins. You will have approximately one hour to prepare. We've arranged for crewmembers to escort you to your superiors. Be ready to present for duty. Any issues, you will, of course, take up with your section commander. Should there be need to take any further action, you will see Commander Myatt. You should only see me if you are a command crewmember or as a point of discipline. I am not one for small talk, so if you present to me, have a very good reason."

He delivered the words slowly and deliberately, and Elara restrained a small smile on hearing at least one gulp from those in the line nearest her.

"We run a tight ship here. Discipline and commitment are the two key factors we look for beyond loyalty in our crew. You will from henceforth represent our ship everywhere, and we do not tolerate anything less than the best." He looked around once more, the stern demeanor he wore so well reinforcing the message. If she hadn't known him for so long, she too might have missed the hint of humor glinting in his eyes, the one many took for coldness.

Her legs ached, and she wanted to move and relieve the pressure on them, but she held herself still, waiting for the command to dismiss. She wouldn't let herself or him down now. Not after she'd worked so long to achieve this position.

As the new ST, she had no previous experience on ships. She had vast experience in the field, but Elara was aware that would count for little in the eyes of most of the crew. She didn't intend to signal a weakness to anyone and least of all on her first day aboard the *Star of Ishtar*. That thought held her still and controlled.

She had big shoes to fill after her predecessor, Jamieson, had retired, even though she knew she could fill the void he'd left behind. As a long-term member of the crew—over twenty years—his tenure on the *Star of Ishtar* had placed him aboard since its launch. Due to his experience in the heat of battle with the Ru'Edan he had made a name for himself as the coldest of cold in the hottest of situations. She hoped to emulate that herself and carve out her own place aboard the Ishtar, as its crew lovingly knew her.

Duvall and Grayson knew how much she wanted to prove herself. They just wouldn't have expected it here, on the Ishtar.

She watched Duvall study her, then, quickly turning on his heel, call to those assembled, "Dismissed."

Once they started to move away, she softened her stance, preparing to turn when the call came.

"Sudonne! A moment if you please."

Elara turned to face Duvall. "Commander?"

"Welcome to the *Star of Ishtar*, Elara. While I am surprised you're the new ST, Grayson and I are pleased you could join us. But how did you manage to pull it off? Keeping it quiet that you were the new

ST?" he asked, his voice deep enough to make most women shiver with anticipation.

She smiled, thinking it was a shame she didn't have any feelings for him except sisterly attachment, but then again, given his lack of deep commitment to women, maybe it wasn't such a shame after all.

She understood what drove him. He wanted his own ship and to captain his own future. They'd spent many nights over wine or ale discussing his beliefs that commitment grounded a person. Inwardly, she shrugged. He'd make those calls for himself, though she was sure that one day he would come across someone who would make him consider his choices a little more thoroughly.

"I'm pleased to be here, Duvall. Having an uncle who happens to be an admiral, he was able to let Captain Elphin know that I wanted to surprise you. It's a small world in the Admiralty. Elphin already knew of me, so he okayed my placement. Once the powers knew there was no impediments to me joining the crew, it was fairly simple from there." She felt a small smile creep onto her face, then let it drop away. "What do you think Grayson thinks?"

"Ah, still chasing him, are you?" He grinned, his eyes twinkling. "I think he'll be pleased you're finally old enough and you're here." He looked her straight in the eye. "But you may just need to remind him of that particular fact." He motioned for her to go before him, barking out a deep laugh. "Come on, I'll show you to your cabin."

Available from Love Books Publishing
Available in Ebook via Books2Read

Direct Autographed Copy
https://www.imogenenix.net/Warriors1

The Blood Bride
Blood Secrets Book 1

Hope just wants to be an ordinary nestling. She went to college and escaped, but now she's back and there's a secret everyone is keeping from her.

Xavier is the new master of the nest, ready to welcome home the daughter of the house who he has never met. He's unprepared for the woman who steals his breath and enchants him.

Now Hope and Xavier must fight for lives and those of the innocents. After all, it is only by overcoming the rogues that they will have a chance of a timeless future together. But will it be in time?

PROLOGUE

As silence descended on the house, the shadows grew—dark grays and blacks that bled into each other. First one figure then another broke away, making a run toward the house. Silent as the grave, they moved swiftly over dew-slicked grass. Then they stopped still. Waiting. Not a movement betrayed them until a signal propelled them back into action and they started crawling upwards. The walls damp coating no barrier to the intruders that ascended in the darkness.

The sound of each window breaking shattered the quiet—the figures were inside. Screams echoed through the night. Yet, in this area of large estates, heavy with noise-absorbing shrubbery, no one could hear those within. The blood-curdling screams went on and on before finally dying away.

Just one sound echoed through the night: The sobbing of a child.

The front door opened and figures trooped out—ghostly spectres against an inky night sky, broken by a single outline. A child in white, carried at the centre of the pack.

No sound broke the silence as they moved toward the trees surrounded the house.

Flames now licked at the manor: A deathly glow of oily smoke rising.

All that remained was a single person—wrapped in a cape of midnight blue beyond the house—watching them melt away.

Jemima moved toward the burning structure, breaking into a run as she breached the threshold. Vainly she attempted to enter, but the heat drove her back.

Now dashing tears from her face, she raced across the graveled driveway toward the gates, where the guardhouse was located. No sign of life existed within the building and some instinct of survival slowed her pace to a careful creep. Out of breath and heaving from exertion, she nervously checked within.

Small puffs of white vapor coloured the glass. She darted from one window to another. Her cloak drawn tightly around her body, hoping it would camouflage her from sight.

Satisfied, Jemima entered through the heavy, wooden front door and moved toward the phone she spied on the floor. Her eyes darting here and there she dialed, listening to the rotary motor as it returned to the proper position. Time was short and if *they* came back, she needed to have shared the message.

The phone rang once. Twice. With a brrping sound it connected.

"Hello?" A male answered and she felt a warm flush of relief at the voice. A voice she knew well.

"The manor has been breached. The girl child taken." The words erupted and her hand trembled.

"On our way." The click of the receiver being replaced echoed loudly in the stillness of the room.

Copper. She smelled copper.

Her stomach soured, knowing it meant more deaths. Jemima looked around for the gun—a gun with deadly, holy water-infused copper bullets—she knew was hidden somewhere in the room. A gun she couldn't find. *No divine intervention exists here*, she thought.

Hopefully *they* didn't remain. Feeding. If they were still here, that's what they would be doing. She found a corner and scrunched down, hiding from sight.

Crouched low, she tried to stay as still as possible, listening for sounds of the vehicles she knew would be coming. She dug her fingers into the flesh of her arms; remaining aware enough to stop before drawing blood. That would surely bring them out. Jemima dragged the cloak around her to capture the warmth, yet there was little to be found.

The sounds of engines roused her from the corner of the room. Jemima inched toward the window, the lead of the old glass distorting her view, hearing raised voices she knew Mistress Cressida had arrived.

Jemima retreated. Remained hidden from the woman because if she knew, all may well be lost. From the shadowed room she listened to the conversation...

"It smells like Estersham." The Mistress' eyes closed. "If it is, we have a problem." She turned once more, her face set and eyes now glacial in intensity. "James?"

The man nodded as if he knew what was to come.

"If I take those steps, I cannot return. Another must stand in my place." Her voice hardened while her eyes glittered in the dim light, piercing in their intensity.

Then the Mistress' voice called out in the near silence. "You and yours have been my loyal servants for so many years. I took an oath to protect you long ago. I renewed it with marriage and births, over and over. Now, my home and yours have been breached and this child taken from us. The girl child, who will be the hope and salvation of our kind, was ripped from the bosom of our nest. I will repay your loyalty and I will get her back." The words of power rippled in the night and licked at Jemima's skin.

Available in Ebook
books2read.com/BloodBride-Nix

Direct Autographed Copy
https://www.imogenenix.net/BloodBride

ALSO BY IMOGENE NIX

<u>**Warriors of the Elector**</u>

- Star of Ishtar
- Starline
- Starfire
- Star of the Fleet
- Starburst
- The Star of Eternity

The Star of Ishtar & Starline - Print

Starfire & Star of the Fleet - Print

Starburst & The Star of Eternity - Print

<u>**Blood Secrets**</u>

- The Blood Bride
- The Illuminated Witch
- The Sorcerer's Touch

<u>**House Secrets (The Blood Secrets Continuation)**</u>

- As Dawn Breaks
- Immortal Consequences
- Book 3 coming 2022

All That Glitters — A House Secrets Novella (coming 2023)

Danu's Secret

- The Downfall of Padraic O'Shaunessy (coming 2023)

The Automaton Series

- Haven House (coming 2022)
- Nobel Crest (coming 2022)
- Unnamed (coming soon)

The Search Duology

- Miss Elspeth's Desire
- Miss Isabelle's Craving

Reunion Trilogy

- War's End
- The Assassin
- Executing Justice

The Reunion Trilogy in Paperback

The Webs Series

- Fated Webs
- Tangled Webs
- Covert Webs

The Webs Series Paperback

21st Testing Protocol

- Cyborg: Redux
- Children Of A Greater Evil
- When Evil Came To Stay
- Finis: The War To End All Wars

<u>**Celtic Cupid Trilogy**</u>

- Blame The Wine
- A Stranger's Embrace
- Revenge On Cupid

The Celtic Cupid Trilogy in Paperback

<u>**Zombieology**</u>

- The Reset (2018 - Love At The End of The World)
- I Dream of Zombies
- The Six Million Dollar Zombie
- Make Room For Zombies (coming 2022)
- Unnamed Zombies novel (coming 2023)

<u>**Knights of Pleasure**</u>

- Silken Knights (coming 2022)

<u>**Single Titles**</u>

The Chocolate Affair (also in Print)

Falling In Love Again (Previously A Sapphire For Karina)

BioCybe (also in Print)

Hesparia's Tears (also in Print)

Tomorrow's Promise

A Bar In Paris (also in Print)

Inheritance Of The Blood (also in Print)

The Plan (also in Print)

Loving Memories (also in Print)

Hero of Heartbreak Hill (also in Print)

My One & Only

Curse Bound (also in Print)

Tia's Redemption (Coming 2022)

Raspberry Dreams (Coming Soon)

Non Fiction

Self Publishing: Absolute Beginners Guide (With Suzi Love)

Written as Ciara Cave

25 Curated Ways To Get Rid Of Telemarketers

Book Signings for Absolute Beginners

ABOUT THE AUTHOR

 Imogene is published in a range of romance genres including Paranormal, Science Fiction and Contemporary. She is mainly published in the UK and USA.

In 2010, Imogene Nix (the pen name not Imogene herself) was born. Imogene sat down and worked tirelessly for 3 months culminating in the book Starline, which became the first in a trilogy titled, "Warriors of the Elector." Since then she's had over 30 titles published and is now focusing on hybridising herself - with a mixture of traditionally published and self-published works.

In fact, she's taking control of many of her back catalogue books, which are slowly re-releasing as self-published titles.

Imogene is a member of a range of professional organisations world wide, and believes in the mantra of mentoring and paying it forward and is actively involved in mentorship (through NaNoWrimo and her vlog: In The Chair With Imogene Nix) and tutoring of new and upcoming authors.

In her spare time she loves to drink coffee, wine & eat chocolate and is parenting her spoiled dog and a ferocious cat along with her husband and 2 human daughters and looks forward to weekends away with her husband in their caravan "The Seven Year Hitch!" Do look forward to her caravan romance at some point!

To Contact Imogene

www.imogenenix.net
imogene@imogenenix.net

facebook.com/ImogeneNix
twitter.com/ImogeneNix
instagram.com/ImogeneNix
bookbub.com/authors/imogenenix

www.ingramcontent.com/pod-product-compliance
Lightning Source LLC
Chambersburg PA
CBHW070312190726
48291CB00012B/1085